Megan

BAYOU SUZETTE

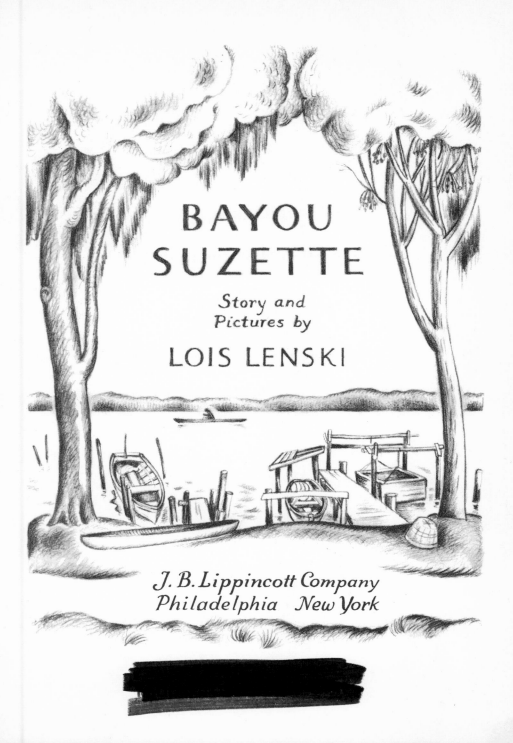

BAYOU SUZETTE

Story and
Pictures by

LOIS LENSKI

J. B. Lippincott Company
Philadelphia   New York

1975

*For
Alex Melançon,
who lives on Bayou Lafourche
but loves
Barataria, too*

CONTENTS

FOREWORD

I AM deeply indebted to many Louisiana friends for generous help in the writing of this story. I wish to thank particularly Alex Melançon, Miss Jeanne B. Peyregne, and Joseph H. Monies, Business Manager of the Jefferson Parish Yearly Review. *The various volumes of this* Review, *from 1936 to 1942, provided a wealth of material, in addition to that which I gathered personally along the banks of Bayou Barataria. Most of all, I wish to thank the many friends I made there, old and young, who so generously and whole-heartedly made my sojourn among them such an enjoyable and memorable experience, and who helped me in every way possible to present this typical picture of Louisiana bayou life.*

All my characters are imaginary, but I have made use of many incidents which were told me by bayou-French people, incidents which had actually happened to them. I have used no real names and in most instances have altered the incidents themselves, for plot purposes.

Certain liberties have been taken with descriptions of the Barataria country to suit the purposes of my story. The Indian mound is actually located at the Berthoud Cemetery, some four miles north of the Bayou des Oies. "Little Village" was the name of a settlement on the opposite side of Bayou Barataria. The village which I have described was named "Lafitte" at a later date than my story.

FOREWORD

I have made use of the recently published Louisiana State Guide Book; "Louisiana-French" by William A. Read; standard works on Jean Lafitte; "Plant Curatives from the Houma Indians" by Frank G. Speck; and Houma material provided by Misses Ella and Wilhelmina Hooper of Dulac, Louisiana.

Barataria will always hold charms because of its many associations with Jean Lafitte, which still survive in fascinating legends. But to me, its greatest charm is and always will be the warmth and sincerity of the bayou-French people themselves.

LOIS LENSKI

New Orleans, Louisiana, December 1941 to April 1942
Greenacres, Harwinton, Connecticut, April 1942 to January 1943

BAYOU SUZETTE

CHAPTER ONE

The Strange Girl

Established 1892
Eugène LeBlanc
General Merchandiser
RAW FURS MOSS & ALLIGATOR HIDES
Bought and Sold

THE SIGN was large and covered the upper half of Père Eugène LeBlanc's store. The words were faint and weather-beaten now, after many years of storm and sunshine. Suzette looked up and read them over, although she knew them well by heart. She set the coal-oil can carefully in the path and pushed her sunbonnet back. She looked at the small bunch of fish strung on a strip of palmetto, which she held in her hand.

"If I had furs now, or moss, or alligator hides, I'd be sure to get coal-oil today," she said aloud. A frown passed over her small, bright face. "Coal-oil makes a better light than coon or fish grease."

The store faced the bayou. It had a wide porch, called a gallery, which reached to the footpath on the low bayou levee. A sharp wind made sprightly waves and whipped them noisily against the shore.

Suzette Durand was ten years old, small, thin and wiry. She wore her hair combed tightly back and braided in one long braid. Dark, bright eyes shone from her oval face, freckles covered her nose and cheeks, her chin was small and pointed.

She picked up her can and stepped up on the gallery. Suddenly the door flew open. A boy rushed out and passed her like a gust of wind.

"Hé! Felix Durand! You leetle animal, come back here!"

Père Eugène, the storekeeper, came running out, bursting with anger. His thin face was red as a turkey-cock's and he waved his arms wildly. He almost jumped out of his shiny green coat.

"You, Felix Durand!" he shouted. "You toad, you snake, you beast! Bring me back those lump of sugar or I tan your hide, me. I tell your Papa, I tell your Maman, I tell your Grandmère how you make shame on the name Durand!"

Suzette shook her head. "He the worstest boy on the by'a." She spoke in the soft patois of the bayou country, which makes "bayou" sound like "by'a."

But Felix did not stop to listen. Laughing with glee, he boldly stuffed several lumps of sugar into his mouth and galloped off along the winding bayou path.

[2]

Père Eugène drew a large red handkerchief from his pocket and mopped his damp face. He buttoned his shiny green coat carefully. Suzette looked up at him. His face was so thin it made his ears stand out on each side. She had never seen him so angry before.

"*Bon jour*, M'sieu'!" she said, with a polite bow.

"That leetle terrible!" sputtered Père Eugène.

"He take somet'ing, M'sieu'?" asked Suzette, gently.

"Take somet'ing! He fill his pocket with pecan or sugar or pepp'mint every time my back, it turned!" cried Père Eugène. "He one wicked thief!"

"*Mais non,* not a thief!" cried Suzette, in a shocked voice. "The Durands, they not steal."

"He a Durand and he take my sugar, I tell you!" snapped Père Eugène. "He fill his pocket full and run off. You see him go."

"I am a Durand and I not take sugar," said Suzette, lifting her chin.

"You may have pride for you," said Père Eugène, "but shame for that cousin of yours. His Maman, she should take a strap to him, yes."

"Poor Tante Henriette!" sighed Suzette. "She got so many children and so leetle time."

She followed Père Eugène into the store, making light tracks in the saw-dust on the floor, and looked around. On shelves behind the counter she saw square glass jars filled with hard, round sugar candy balls, tiny striped peppermint sticks and sugar hearts with mottoes. On the counter itself stood a great yellow cheese, with a wedge cut out of one side, and also the box of lump sugar which Felix had sampled. Kitchen utensils sat on the floor beside large coils of rope, while from the ceiling dangled an array of muskrat traps. A barrel of dried shrimp in a corner gave out a sharp aroma, competing with the odor of dried apples and peaches near by.

Suzette's eyes swept the interior in a glance, then she stared. For sitting on the floor beside a barrel of sugar cane syrup, she saw a strange girl of the same age as herself.

[4]

"Another animal!" scolded Père Eugène, pointing. "W'at have I not suffered this day!" He threw up his hands in great agitation. "There she sit all the time and wait. She do not'ing but wait. She not go—I can't shoo her out. W'at she want, only *le bon Dieu,* the good God, he know. She not speak, she not answer questions. She just sit. Her black eyes, they follow me every place I go and me, I don't like it. If she don't get outa here, I go crazy. Me, I can't stand it no longer."

Suzette always liked Père Eugène's store. It was the only store along the bayou front and things always happened there. Neighbors were always coming in, talking and laughing, and she could tell Papa Jules and Maman about it when she got home. A visit to Père Eugène's store was always worth while.

But today there was only a strange girl with black hair, crouched against a syrup barrel. Suzette was disappointed to see none of the people she knew. She stared at the girl and the girl stared back at her. Then she went to the counter and handed her bunch of fish to Père Eugène.

"Two bits," he said briefly, meaning a quarter.

"Papa Jules say, he want nails, M'sieu'," said Suzette. "Enough to make a crab car."

Père Eugène dropped a handful of nails onto the scales, then slid them into a paper sack.

"Your Papa, he feel well again? He feel like makin' a crab car? He go crab fishin' soon?"

"My Papa, he sit up every day, M'sieu'," said Suzette, proudly, "and yesterday, he make one big walk across the room, him."

" 'Bout time he sit up! 'Bout time he walk! 'Bout time he work again, him!" said the storekeeper, with a frown. "W'at else you want, Mam'selle?"

"How much I got left, M'sieu'?" asked Suzette.

"Eighteen cent."

"My Maman say, she want plenty coffee today."

Père Eugène put coffee in a paper bag. "Thirteen cent," he said.

"And plenty sugar and plenty grease," said Suzette.

Père Eugène put up two very small packages of sugar and lard.

"Now how much left?" asked Suzette.

"Not'ing. Your money, it all spent."

"But my Papa say, he want plenty tobacco," said Suzette, "and my Maman say, she want coal-oil to burn in the lamp." She lifted the can up to the counter.

"Not today," said Père Eugène, firmly. "Your money, it all spent, I tell you. Better catch more feesh tomorrow."

"But Papa Jules, he say . . ."

"You all the time askin' for t'ings for your Papa," growled Père Eugène.

"Only a leetle tobacco," begged Suzette, "when he got to lie in bed all day . . . and the bullet inside him hurt so much . . ."

"W'y the doctor, he not take the bullet out?" demanded Père Eugène.

"He take one out, but he can't find the other one," explained Suzette.

"Well, if your Papa had stay home from the shootin' match, he not get shot!" shouted Père Eugène, angrily. "If he let Claude Broussard alone, he not now have one bullet in his back!"

"But plenty, plenty people 'long the by'a goes when there is a shootin' match, M'sieu' Gene," protested Suzette, loyally. "Nobody stay home, you know that. You close up your store and go yourself, and my Papa, he the best shot 'long the by'a! He hit the mark, he win the bigges', fattes' pig and we eat him up and he taste good. You not like pork chop, M'sieu'?"

"Time your Papa get to work to support his family," said Père Eugène, gruffly. "W'y he not get outa bed and go fishin', trappin' and huntin'?"

"With a bullet in his back, M'sieu'?" Suzette's eyes were soft with gentle reproach.

"How his wife and children gonna eat then?"

"We en't starve yet, M'sieu' Gene!" said Suzette, with a toss of her head. "My Nonc Lodod and my Nonc Moumout and my Nonc Serdot, they all the time take good care of us. My brother, Ambrose, he like to go fishin' and huntin', him. Me, I fish fish every day. I got patience, me, to fish. I swap the fish for the coffee, the sugar, the grease . . ."

She paused, thoughtfully. "Papa Jules, he got plenty mouth to feed, yes. He got Grandmère to feed, and Maman and Ambrose, and my big sister Eulalie, and me and my three leetle brothers . . ."

"And all the lazy-bone neighbors, eh?" added Père Eugène. "So that w'y you need so much coffee, to keep the coffee-pot all the time runnin' over!"

"When our frien's they come to call, M'sieu', we give coffee to drink," said Suzette, with dignity. "We not too poor to be polite."

Suzette Durand was used to defending her father before Père Eugène and before neighbors and relations as well. Many of the people along Bayou Barataria thought that twenty-two months was too long for a man to lie abed with a bullet in his back and that it was time for Jules Durand to show himself a man and get up. But Père Eugène had never been so fierce, so outspoken as today. Suzette's hand trembled as she lifted the empty coal-oil can down and picked up the paper sacks.

She turned to go.

Then she saw the strange girl again. Her face was dark and very dirty. Her hair was black and straight, her clothes torn and ragged. But the look of fear on her face was somehow mixed with wonder and trust.

"Who are you?" asked Suzette.

The girl stared hard but did not speak.

"Who *are* you?" Suzette repeated the question.

"Me, I tell you who she is," shouted Père Eugène, from behind the counter. "She one of them good-for-nothing half-breed Indians from the back country. First I see her standin' on the wagon road 'cross the by'a with a dirty ole Indian woman, sellin' baskets. I buy one or two, then she start comin' here. Now she bring no more baskets, no. She hang round all the time and me, I can't shoo her off. She one leetle animal, like all her tribe."

"W'at your name?" asked Suzette, gently.

"Mar-teel!" the two syllables were little more than a whisper.

"Marteel? Marteel w'at?" asked Suzette.

"Marteel, me!" said the Indian girl, pointing to herself.

"Where you live?" asked Suzette.

The girl shook her head.

"You got no home, no? No bed to sleep in?"

Again she shook her head.

"You got no maman, no papa?" asked Suzette.

Another shake.

"No grandmère? No grandpère? No great-grandmère and no great-grandpère in the graveyard?"

"Don't worry!" shouted Père Eugène. "She got father and mother and plenty brother and sister and uncle and aunt and cousin. The Injuns, they're like the antses. Where there one, there a flock."

"You got no maman?" Suzette's eyes opened wide at such an impossibility.

Marteel looked very sad. She shook her head again and in her eyes there came a look of pleading.

"My Maman is a beautiful to take care of somebody," said Suzette, softly. "My Papa Jules, he is shot in the back and didn't get well yet. Marteel come home with me, yes."

The Indian girl rose and followed her.

"Another mouth for Papa Jules to feed!" cried Père Eugène, with a chuckle. "Well, *I* get rid of her, anyhow."

"Ho, there, you, Suzette!" he shouted, suddenly, coming to the door behind her. "Here somet'ing for you. You forgot your lagniappe." He handed out two tiny striped peppermint sticks.

It was customary after a purchase for a storekeeper to make a generous gesture and offer some trifle as a gift.

"Oh no, no, M'sieu'," said Suzette, drawing back. "No, *merci*, M'sieu', I couldn't take no pepp'mint stick today, M'sieu'!"

"Not even for your leetle brothers, no?" asked Père Eugène.

To Suzette's little brothers, candy was always a special treat. But after the refusal of tobacco for her sick father and Père Eugène's harsh words, Suzette's pride would not let her accept the gift. The storekeeper's new generosity could not heal the hurt he had given her.

"No, *merci*, M'sieu'!" repeated Suzette coldly. "Come, we go home, Marteel."

On the bayou path, the Indian girl stopped abruptly.

"See!" she said. She pulled her ragged shirt down over one shoulder to show her bared neck. She pointed with a dirty brown finger. "It hurt, but well now." Running down the girl's back, Suzette saw great red, lumpy scars. "Ole squaw push burning splinters under the skin," Marteel explained.

"O-o-o-h, no!" cried Suzette, in horror. "Who would do a thing like that?"

"Ole squaw. Ole Injun squaw," answered Marteel.

"Your . . . your grandmère?"

"No, no got grandmère," said Marteel. "Ole squaw."

Suzette's eyes showed horror and sympathy. All she could say was, "Marteel come home with me, yes."

She started off and the Indian girl followed.

The houses along the bayou were set close together in neighborly fashion. Each had its own small front yard and fence. A winding footpath ran in and out and up and down on the low levee between the fences and the water's edge. Chinaberry and hackberry trees and young live-oaks made sun-speckled patches of shade. Each house had its own wharf at the edge of the bayou, and beside the wharves, pirogues, skiffs and a few sailing luggers were moored.

Suzette's bare feet pattered lightly along the dirt path, but the Indian girl's footsteps behind her made no sound. The wind was blowing harder now and the water made rhythmical gurgles as it slapped against the levee bank. Here and there the soil had been washed away in great bites, leaving steep, straight embankments down to the water's surface. Where the path itself had been washed out, planks were laid across for narrow bridges.

Suzette pointed out the various houses. "The Bergerons, they live here," she said. "They got a boy name' Theophile and a girl name' Beulah. The Broussards live next. They got two girls, Elise and Ellen Elaine, but we don't speak to them no more."

"*Bon jour*, M'sieu' and Madame Theriot," she said, politely, as they passed an old couple sitting on a bench beside the path. "They live in there. Their grandchildren are name' René and Doreen Dugas. Now we come to the Durands. The by'a, it full of Durands. Tante Céleste, she live here by herself. Nonc Lodod, he rich, he buy the house for her. She don't like to live by other people."

They walked on. She pointed out her uncles' houses.

"Tante Henriette and Nonc Serdot, they live here," said Suzette. "They got fifteen children, only some are dead and some married. That bad Felix, he their boy, and Odalia, Olivia and Ophelia, they some of his sisters.

"Now we come to Nonc Lodod and Tante Thérèse. They got a phonograph and white paint on their house, and a fine new house-boat."

The two girls stopped again.

"Tante Toinette and Nonc Moumout live here. Tante Toinette, she like cats, and Nonc Moumout, he spend all his time fishing."

Marteel, the Indian girl, had listened to all of Suzette's chatter, but had said nothing. They came to their last stop.

"This where my Maman and my Papa Jules live," said Suzette, proudly. "And my Grandmère and my big sister Eulalie and Ambrose and my three leetle brothers."

She stopped before a small frame house of a faded orange color, with a built-in front gallery or porch. A steep stairway rose from the gallery to the *grenier* or attic bedroom. The front of the house had two doors, tightly closed with solid batten shutters, made to swing outward.

"My Grandpère, he build this house when he marry my Grandmère," Suzette announced solemnly. "Now, my Grandpère, he dead and buried in the graveyard, but Grandmère, she live with us."

She opened the gate. Three dogs came running out, two hounds and a small house dog. "Papa's hunting dogs are name' Roro and Toto, and this is leetle Poo-poo," Suzette explained. She patted the small dog on the head. "They won't hurt you. Come in, Marteel. Come and see my Maman."

The Indian girl hung back. She looked up and down the bayou as if she wanted to run away.

Suzette heard voices coming from the house.

"Wait here," she said. "I go see."

She went into the yard and stopped beneath a window. The window had no glass sash or frame, but a wide batten shutter which opened out. Suzette listened for a moment to the voices inside. Then she went round to the kitchen door and set the oil can and the packages on the back doorstep.

Returning, she took Marteel by the hand. "Come," she said. She led her to a clump of bushes in the back yard, behind a shed. "Sit down," she ordered. "Wait here till I come."

"Marteel wait, yes," said the Indian girl.

CHAPTER TWO

The Skiff Peddlers

SUZETTE took her purchases in and put them on the kitchen table. She listened again to the voices in the front room.

"Every fisherman, if he worth his salt, he own his own boat," her mother was saying. "All Jules' brothers, they got boats. Every man along the by'a got his own boat. How we ever gonna get along . . ."

Her mother was scolding again. Suzette knew this was no time to bring in the Indian girl.

"But the hard times, they come to us all." This was Grandmère's soft voice. "The worst it over now, Clothilde. We must be patient, yes. Soon Jules he be hisself again."

"Soon! Soon! Soon!" cried Suzette's mother, in vexation. "You been sayin' that since the by'a had ice! For twenty-two month you been sayin' *soon,* and he never even try to get outa bed. He lazy, that w'at!"

Her father said nothing in his own defense. Suzette could hear the bed creak and she knew he was turning his face to the wall. No, she could never bring the Indian girl in at a time like this. Much as she loved her mother, her heart burned with sympathy for her father. Maman was cruel today—Maman, who knew how to be so kind.

Jacques, Joseph and little Noonoo came running into the kitchen. "W'at you bring us from de store?" they cried. "Somet'ing good?"

"Not'ing," she answered hastily. "Not'ing for you."

She went into the bedroom.

"W'at you get today, Suzette?" asked her mother, sharply.

"Nails and leetle bitty coffee and sugar and grease," she said.

Papa Jules turned over and looked at her. His face was pale and unshaven. His eyes brightened. "And tobacco, *ma petite?*"

"M'sieu' Gene en't give me eny today, Papa," said Suzette, sadly. "No coal-oil. No pepp'mint. No tobac'. He say, the money, it en't enough. Tomorrow I ketch two bunch fish, me."

"Père Eugène, he gittin' stingy, him," said Papa Jules. He turned his face to the wall again.

The Indian girl waited as patiently under the bushes as she had waited in the store. She waited for the rest of the day. Once when Suzette ran out to throw some scraps to the chickens, she handed her a piece of bread. "Wait!" she said again.

To Suzette, the day seemed the longest she had ever

known, but it came to an end at last. Night brought bedtime. Maman put little Noonoo to bed beside Papa Jules. Jacques and Joseph clattered up the front ladder stairs to their attic bedroom. Ambrose soon followed.

There were two small bedrooms in the main part of the house. The one opening into the kitchen belonged to Maman and Papa Jules. The other had a double bed, shared by Grandmère and Eulalie, and a cot for Suzette.

After Suzette went to bed, it seemed as if her elders would never come. Eulalie took a long time getting undressed and fixing her hair. When Grandmère came, it seemed as if she would never lie still, but at last her steady snoring began.

Suzette pushed the mosquito bar aside and crept out of bed softly. The room was very dark, because the batten shutter was kept tightly closed. She felt her way, unhooked the door onto the front gallery and went out. The moon was shining and she could see clearly in the yard.

Under the bushes sat Marteel, still waiting.

"Come," said Suzette.

The Indian girl followed her into the house, and without undressing, crept into the cot beside her.

Morning came quickly—all too quickly.

"*Ma bonté!*" cried Eulalie, rising on one elbow. "Look yonda, Grandmère, see w'at Suzette got!"

Grandmère rubbed her eyes and looked. "Hé, Susu!" she cried, in astonishment.

Quickly Suzette pulled the red-checkered quilt over Marteel's head. She had meant to rise before daylight and hide the Indian girl under the bushes again. Now it was too late.

Eulalie rushed over to the cot and pulled the quilt back. "Look!" she screamed. "See w'at Suzette got!"

"Do-o-o-n't, Lala!" cried Suzette. "Let 'er be!"

Grandmère rose slowly from the creaking bed. Maman came to the door and all the boys crowded in. Then suddenly, behind them, there stood Papa Jules.

"*Bonté!*" "W'at Suzette got?" "Lemme see!" "W'at Suzette got?" The room resounded with astonished cries. "Look, she got a Sabine in her bed."

Suzette jumped up in her nightgown and stood by Marteel's side. She grasped the girl's hand and held it tightly. Maman chased the boys back into the kitchen.

"A Sabine! *Ma foi!*" exclaimed Eulalie. "A dirty Injun sleepin' in her bed!"

"W'at in the name o' sense do you mean, Suzette . . ." began Maman.

"Who is it, *ma petite?*" asked Papa Jules, gently. "Where she come from? Tell us."

"Me, I find her by Père Eugène." Suzette swallowed hard to make the words come. "M'sieu' Gene, he say, she sell baskets but he don't like her to look with her black eyes at him all day. He shoo her out . . ."

"I should t'ink so!" interrupted Maman.

"W'at else, *ma petite?*" asked Papa Jules.

"She en't got no maman, no papa, no brothers and sisters, no grandmère, no grandpère!" cried Suzette, passionately. "She en't got no home to go to, no bed to sleep in, she en't got not'ing to eat, she got only one name, and the ole Injun squaw . . ."

"She gotta go back to the ole squaw," said Maman, sternly. "Back where she come from."

"But the ole squaw . . ." began Suzette, trying to explain about the scars.

"Jes' look w'at she done to the clean sheet!" shrilled Eulalie. "She en' even wash her feetses! And she en' even took off her clothes—she slep' in her dirty rags!"

"She my frien' . . ." began Suzette, feebly.

Grandmère and Papa Jules stood by the door and said nothing. Suzette looked toward them longingly.

"Dirty no-count Injun!" exclaimed Maman. "I declare, Suzette, I don't know w'at you t'inkin' 'bout, to bring a dirty savage in your nice clean bed. We don't want her here. We got big enough family as 'tis. She gotta go."

"But . . . but . . . she en't got no maman . . . to go to," wailed Suzette. "She en't got no bed to sleep in!"

"Oh, plenty Injun lives in the woods where she come from," said Maman. "She be all right."

The girl did not stir. She held tightly to Suzette's hand, looking from one face to the other, bewildered.

Maman walked briskly out to the kitchen and returned with the broom. "Now you git right out, and don't let me ever see you round here again." She opened the door onto the front gallery, but the Indian girl did not budge.

Maman put down her broom, surprised. "Tell her to go, Suzette." The Indian girl seemed to mind no one but Suzette.

Suzette gave one despairing glance in the direction of Grandmère and Papa Jules.

At last Papa Jules spoke. "Maman, she right, Susu," he said. "We can't pick up all the basket-selling Indians in the woods. They'd eat us outa house and home."

Suzette let the girl's hand drop.

"Go!" she said, in a low voice.

The Indian girl walked out the door.

That day, Suzette sat hunched disconsolately on the

wharf in front of her home. The flies, gnats and mosquitoes nipped her bare arms and legs. The sun shone furiously hot. The bayou was as still as a mirrored lake. She baited her lines but she caught no fish.

The next day she had better luck.

"Maman," she announced, "I take the skiff today and sell my fish by M'sieu' Guidry, across the by'a."

"Across the by'a, *mais non!*" cried Maman. "W'at you t'ink, Suzette! Me, I die of fright to see you alone in the skiff. You drown yourself like little Tit-tit. You can't never go in the skiff alone. You take your fish to Père Eugène like you all the time do."

"It too hot to walk so far," complained Suzette.

"But Suzette, you like all the time to go by Père Eugène," said Maman.

"Me, I let Felix row the skiff," suggested Suzette.

"That leetle terrible? And dump you in the by'a?"

"I don't wanna go by Père Eugène no more," wailed Suzette. "He en't give me tobac' for my Papa."

"Clothilde, let her go 'cross the by'a if she want to!" thundered Papa Jules from the bedroom.

" 'Cross the by'a? In the skiff? Alone?" cried Maman. "Oh, my pore leetle Suzette! She is drown' already, like pore leetle Tit-tit! Oh, it a cruel Papa she has, to t'ink of such a t'ing."

"Ambrose can row her over," said Papa Jules, quietly. "Suzette, she not buy groceries from now on, she keep her

fish money for her own self. Ambrose, he take his fish to
Père Eugène for the groceries."

"Me, I die of fright!" cried Maman. "I die of fright!"

Maman was so upset she did not even trust careful
Ambrose. She leaned far out over the pot-shelf where she
was washing dishes and cried: "Be careful, Ambrose!
Don't tip the skiff and drown your sister, Ambrose!"

Maman was wide and fat. She leaned hard on the dish-
pan and tipped it so the water ran all over the front of her
dress and apron. It ran over the pot-shelf and down to the
ground.

So Suzette no longer went to Père Eugène's store. Each
day Suzette and Ambrose fished fish and fished crabs and
then Ambrose rowed her across the bayou. Ambrose was
fourteen years old and big and strong. He was a dark-
faced, quiet boy, with sad eyes. He worked hard, played
little and never had much to say. He could handle a
pirogue or a skiff as well as a man, and was trying hard to
fill his father's place.

Monsieur Guidry was kind—he was a good friend of
Papa Jules. He had a sugar-cane plantation on the other
side of the bayou. He bought all of Suzette's catch without question and paid her generously. Each day when she
came home, she put the coins in a little box which she
kept under her mattress. Suzette saved every penny, for
she knew that Marteel would some day be back and she
laid her plans carefully.

It was across the bayou that she found the Indian girl
again. One day, after selling her fish, she saw a figure
standing at the edge of the woods.

"Marteel! Marteel!" cried Suzette.

Ambrose said nothing, but when they came back to the skiff, he balked. "En't takin' no Injun girl 'cross the by'a!" he announced.

"Please, Ambrose!" begged Suzette. "She en't got no home nor no maman . . ."

"Our Maman, she say she don't want no dirty Injun 'round the house," said Ambrose, stubbornly. "You comin' home?"

"If Marteel can't come, me, I stay by her," said Suzette.

Without a word, Ambrose picked up the oars and rowed across the bayou. Suzette watched. She saw him pull up at the wharf in front of their home. The houses along the bayou front had never looked so small before, and the bayou itself had never looked so wide.

Suzette looked at Marteel. "You swim?" she asked.

"Yes, Marteel swim like a fish," said the Indian girl, with a smile.

"Me, I can't," said Suzette. "My Maman, she don't want me to swim in the by'a, 'count of all the gar-fish to bite me."

So they could not get across by swimming.

They sat on the soggy bank. There was no levee on this side and the shore was wet and muddy. Suzette looked down at the mud on her legs and feet.

"My Maman's gonna *run* me, if she see all this mud."

She dipped her feet in the water and washed them off.

The Indian girl did the same.

"We'll shout!" said Suzette. "Somebody will hear and come for us. I t'ink my Papa, he sit in a rocking chair on the front gallery today. He hear us and send Ambrose back."

But Ambrose did not come. It was another, larger skiff that picked them up and took them across. There were two men in it. They heard Suzette's shouts and pulled in by the shore.

"The dish-pan peddlers!" cried Suzette, joyfully. "It's 'Tit Pierre and Gros Paul! I en't seen them for a long time, I en't."

Little Peter and Big Paul were brothers, well known up and down the bayous. In their skiff they carried a variety of dry-goods, shoes, notions, cooking pots and dish-pans. Little Peter was small and thin, Big Paul large and fat. Little Peter did the buying and selling. Big Paul rowed the skiff and did whatever Little Peter told him to.

"*Bonté!*" cried 'Tit Pierre, in surprise. "If it en't Mam'selle Suzette Durand herself, perched over here on the edge of the by'a like a leetle lost prairie chick!"

"Oh, M'sieu' Pierre!" cried Suzette. "Please take us over. Ambrose my brother, he went back in the skiff and left us."

Gros Paul stood staring at the Indian girl.

"Git in," said 'Tit Pierre. "We was aimin' to stop by your house when we hear you callin'. First I thought you had fell in, then I saw you was up on shore."

Suzette stepped in.

"We take her too?" asked Gros Paul, pointing to Marteel with his thumb.

"She stayin' by me, to my house," explained Suzette, hastily.

"Git in, then," said 'Tit Pierre.

Marteel stepped in and the two girls sat down on the piles of dry-goods. It did not take long to cross. Gros Paul slid his skiff up beside the wharf and moored it. Ambrose was not in sight, nor was his skiff. Papa Jules was not on the front gallery. No one was to be seen up or down the bayou path. Little Village seemed to be taking its afternoon nap.

Gros Paul picked up a large tin dish-pan, pounded on it with an iron spoon and made a loud banging. The sleepy houses suddenly woke up. People opened their front doors and looked. Children and barking dogs came running. A group of boys collected, Felix and Jacques among them.

"I go find my Maman," said Suzette. "She never like to miss you, M'sieu' Pierre. My Maman say, she want to buy lace and buttons for my big sister Lala's new dress."

The visit of the skiff peddlers was always an event. Père Eugène did not sell much dry-goods or many notions at his store. He preferred trading with the men in furs, moss and alligator hides. He had little patience with women and their needs. The skiff peddlers, on the other hand, came straight from New Orleans, twenty odd miles to the northward, with the very latest printed calicoes and trinkets chosen to please the ladies of the bayous.

But, exciting as their visit was, Suzette did not lose her head completely. Not for a single minute did she forget her new friend, Marteel. She knew she must get her out of sight before all the customers came.

"Come with me. Quick, Marteel!" she called.

Felix and Jacques stared at the Indian girl as she climbed out of the skiff. Suzette ran swiftly with her round the house till they came to the clump of bushes back of the shed.

"Wait!" she said, as before.

The girl crouched down and waited.

Suzette hurried into the house, but both Maman and Grandmère were gone. Papa Jules was asleep in his bed. The banging of the dish-pan had not wakened him. Suzette tiptoed past, went to her cot and, taking out her money box, counted the coins. Then she hurried out to the wharf again.

"My Maman and my Grandmère, they not at home," she told 'Tit Pierre. "They gone by my Tante Thérèse to sew Lala's new dress on her sewing machine. You know M'sieu' Lodod Durand, yes?"

"All the ladies together!" nodded 'Tit Pierre. "It good, that. We sell out everyt'ing, we empty the skiff!"

Gros Paul untied the rope and took up the oars.

"But wait! Don't go yet!" cried Suzette. "Me, I want somet'ing."

"W'at!" laughed 'Tit Pierre. "I almost miss a sale. W'at you want, young leddy, today?"

"Me, I want eight yard bed ticking . . . enough to make a mattress cover . . ." she stammered, "and ten yard cheesecloth for a mosquito bar . . ." She handed her money to the peddler. "It money enough?"

"W'at! Real money?" joked 'Tit Pierre. "No hides to-

day? No mink and coon skins? Suzette, she gettin' rich, *n'est pas?*"

Gros Paul roared loudly as he measured off the cloth.

"It . . . it money enough?" asked Suzette.

"Just right! How you figger it out?" 'Tit Pierre looked at the money before he put it in his pocket, then he added, soberly, "You en't steal this, Mam'selle, no?"

"Oh no, M'sieu' Pierre!" Suzette's chin went up. "Me, a Durand, I don't steal not'ing. Me, I fish fish and fish crab and M'sieu' Guidry, he give me cash money for it."

"Ver' good," said 'Tit Pierre, as the skiff moved away from the wharf.

Suzette took the ticking and the cheesecloth and ran back to the shed. She hid the bundles away in a dark corner behind a barrel of muskrat traps. Her plans were working out nicely.

She ran to the kitchen, found a loaf of bread and stuffed it in a paper sack. Then she joined the waiting Indian girl.

"Come, Marteel!" she said. "Now our chance, while ev'body 'long the by'a is watchin' the skiff peddlers. You paddle a pirogue, yes?"

Marteel nodded. "Like a bird over the water."

"We go in the pirogue to the swamp," said Suzette.

CHAPTER THREE

The Cypress Swamp

MARTEEL showed no surprise and she needed no urging. She was more at home in a pirogue than walking on land. It was the Indians who first hollowed out a log of wood by burning it with fire, then shaped it into the form of a shallow flat canoe rising no more than three inches above the water, and called it a dug-out. Marteel, like all Indians, had been born to the art of handling a pirogue.

The skiff peddlers had moved on up the bayou and were now in front of Nonc Lodod's house. The crowd of women and children had moved along with them. All but Felix and Jacques, who, knee-deep in the water beside the wharf, had caught an eel and were trying to put it in a big rusty tin.

The long slender pirogue, with Marteel's hand on the paddle, moved silently out into the bayou in long sweeps. So lightly did it move, it seemed scarcely to touch the water at all.

"Where you goin', Suzette?" shouted Felix, letting the eel slip out of his hands.

"Who takin' you off in the pirogue, Suzette?" cried
Jacques, staring.

But Suzette did not answer.

Marteel headed down stream, away from the village.
Suzette took out the loaf of bread, broke it in two and
gave half to the Indian girl. But she let it lie beside her
and did not eat. Kneeling comfortably on the curved
bottom of the pirogue, her eyes fixed straight ahead, she
raised and lowered the flashing paddle. Past low shores of
waving marsh grass and reeds, past patches of bristling,
sun-splashed palmetto, past thorny vine-hung brambles
the pirogue moved.

Suzette did not tell Marteel where to go. She seemed to
be well acquainted with the Barataria waterways, with
the salt-grass flats as well as the swamps farther inland.
Soon she turned away from the bayou into a side canal.
It took only a few moments for the pirogue to plunge
from bright sunshine into the dark shadows of the swamp.

"Oh, how fast you paddle!" cried Suzette.

Marteel did not answer.

Now the forest came down to the very banks of the
stream. Tall cypress trees, rooted below water and braced
fanlike to resist both wind and flood, humped up their
wooden "knees" on all sides, to give breath to their roots
below. Their lofty, stiff branches above were draped in
long streamers of gray Spanish moss. Here and there the
sun splashed through, lighting up the shadows and mak-

ing ghostlike reflections in the stagnant water.

"We pick moss in the swamp," said Suzette, explaining her errand. "We pick plenty moss. We make a bed for Marteel to sleep in."

"A bed for me?" laughed Marteel, unbelieving. "My bed, it the damp ground, the winding stream, the branch of the oak tree, the wet swamp! I sleep enywhere, me!"

"My Papa, he used to be a moss picker," Suzette went on. "Before he got shot, he pick moss every day. He soak it and hang it on the fence to dry. Then he sell it to Père Eugène for the groceries. We have all the time plenty groceries to eat then."

Above their heads and on all sides as far as they could see, the ghostly gray moss dropped in never-ending curtains. Both girls knew it well. To the French girl, moss was something to sell, but to the Indian girl it was a gift to stir the imagination. She began to speak in a low voice.

"Marteel, she belong to the tribe of the Houmas. The Indians name themselves 'Houmas'—the People-of-the-Rising-Sun." She reached for a low-hanging strand of moss and twined it round her head like a crown. "The Houmas, they have their own name for the moss—they call it Gray-Hair-Falling-Down."

Suzette was surprised to hear Marteel speak so plainly. She had used only halting words before.

"Papa Jules, he say the French people name it Spanish-beard, 'cause the Spanish people bring it. The Spanish people, they name it French-wig, 'cause they say the French people bring it. The French and the Spanish, they not love each other. Each blame the other for the moss. W'y the Indians name it Gray-Hair-Falling-Down?"

"The Houmas, they like to tell how it got its name," replied Marteel. "Long, long ago, a Houma princess was kill' by the enemy on her wedding day. Her people, they bury her beneath a big, big oak tree. They have an old custom—they cut off the bride's hair and they hang it on a limb. A storm, it come in the night, but it not blow the bride's hair away. The hair, it start to grow where it hang. Many moons they go by—the black hair it turn gray. It grow and it grow. It spread from the oak tree to the cypress tree. It spread all through the great forest— Gray-Hair-Falling-Down all through the forest."

Marteel paused thoughtfully, then went on. "The Houmas, they pull the moss from the trees and use it too. They dry the inside fibers and twist them to make a strong rope that never break. The ole Injun squaw, she weave the moss fibers on a wooden frame over and under, she make big mat for the floor of her palmetto house."

Marteel's voice faded away.

Suddenly a blue heron flashed across the pirogue's path. Then above the even sounds of the paddle strokes, mysterious noises could be heard, squawkings, gruntings, rustlings and chirpings. Before Suzette knew it, they were deep in the cypress swamp. She looked about her and knew they had come a long way.

Every bayou child knows the swamps as well as he knows the sunny streams, the winding bayous, the boggy marshes and the wet prairies of Louisiana. But a sudden fear gripped the heart of Suzette. At that moment she realized for the first time that an Indian girl might know them far better than a white child ever could. In the woods, in the swamp, Marteel was a different creature

Here she came truly alive. What was it she had said about her bed being in the wet swamp? Did she really mean it?

Now the sun hid its face and the swamp grew darker and more strange. The chorus of weird noises pressed closer on Suzette's ear. She shivered with fear. Where was the Indian girl taking her?

"Marteel!" she cried aloud. "Me, I don't like to go so far. We gotta have solid ground to step on or we can't pick moss. All round here, it water. Me, I don't like the smelly water with the green scum on top, I wanna go back!"

"Green scum!" exclaimed Marteel. "You don't know w'at it is? The buds from the trees, they fall down on the water, that w'at it is." She laid her paddle down. "Listen!" she said, cupping her hand to her ear.

"W'at you hear?" asked Suzette. "Me, I hear frogs croaking."

"Marteel, she hear w'at the birds say to each other," replied the Indian girl. "Marteel, she hear w'at the wind say when it blow softly through the trees and shake the leaves. Marteel, she hear w'at the animals, her brothers, tell each other. All the wild animals they Marteel's brothers. Marteel, she talk to them, she listen to all they say."

"But I can't hear all that, me," said Suzette. "I hear croaking and twittering and grunting, but I can't tell w'at they sayin'."

"No!" said Marteel. "The savage hears best, because he

loves the swamp, the forest. He never 'fraid."

The silence was broken now by the louder croakings of alligators and the raucous screams of swamp fowls.

"Now I show you where my friend, brother Alligator, lives," said Marteel, taking up the paddle again.

"*Mais non!*" cried Suzette, shrinking back. "Me, I only want to pick moss for your bed."

The pirogue moved silently along a devious passage, dodging cypress knees and slipping around fern-covered tree trunks.

"Brother Bear, he live here," said Marteel, pulling up close beside the hollowed-out bole of a huge root-sunken cypress. She picked up a handful of dry leaves and let them fall. "He not home today. He not here to talk to us. He not been here for a long time—mebbe he dead."

The pirogue moved on through the glassy, unruffled water. The long streamers of moss hung motionless. The air was still. Marteel rested her paddle and the pirogue drifted. The sun, shining again, sifted through in fanlike slits. Marteel's face glowed with a strange light. Was it only the sun's reflection or was it the radiance of happiness?

Suzette looked at her and was ashamed of her former fears. She was safer in the swamp with Marteel than with anyone else, just because she knew it so well.

Marteel pushed the pirogue along slowly.

"Right here the alligators live," she said, pointing to

the bank. A litter of about fifty eggs, arranged in three layers in a mound of earth, moss and grass, lay exposed to the sun among the grasses and brambles at the water's edge.

"Alligator eggs!" cried Suzette. "If Ambrose, he see 'em . . ."

"Listen!" interrupted Marteel.

"W'at you hear?" asked Suzette.

"People coming. Voices." Marteel pushed on farther.

The laughing voices came closer and soon a skiff appeared. In it were Ambrose, Jacques and Felix.

"We followed you," explained Felix. "We watched where you went. We tole Ambrose and he come too."

"W'at you come out here with that Injun girl for?" demanded Ambrose. "All this long way in the swamp? We almost lose ourself a hundred time. W'at you come here for?"

"To pick moss," said Suzette.

"Plenty moss nearer home," growled Ambrose. "No need to come so far. Maman, she not want you to come to the swamp. W'y you en't mind our Maman? Come, we gotta go home."

"Me, I en't goin'," said Suzette, stubbornly. "Not till I get my moss, I en't."

"You better come quick! Plenty alligator round here," Ambrose went on. "Papa he come here plenty time on alligator hunt. You wanna see alligator?"

"I see a 'gator's nest right back there," said Suzette.

"Where?" cried Ambrose, suddenly all eagerness.

"Where?" cried the other boys. "We get the eggs. We take 'em home."

The shore was solid land to step on. Ambrose and Felix jumped out of the skiff and ran to the nest.

"We take 'em home and hatch 'em," cried Felix. "We feed 'em and raise a whole flock of 'gators in a tin tub."

The boys took off their caps, filled them with alligator eggs and carried them back to the skiff. Meanwhile, Suzette jumped out of the pirogue and Marteel followed. Like a flying squirrel, Marteel slipped up a large tree, darted about among its branches and pulled loose great streamers of moss, dropping them at Suzette's feet. Soon the boys, too, were in the trees and the moss was falling in showers. Their happy shouts rang through the forest and blotted out all the strange and unfamiliar noises.

On the ground, Jacques and Suzette began gathering up piles of moss so large they could scarcely stagger under the load.

"We fill the skiff, too!" cried Suzette, happily. "Ambrose, you swap some by Père Eugène for Maman's groceries. Then she not scold."

The boys came down and helped to load. Felix made a great pile in the stern of the skiff, jumping on the spongy mass to press it down. Jacques made a smaller one in the bow, leaving room in the center of the boat for Ambrose

to row, and for the alligator eggs at his feet.

"Jacques and me, we ride on top!" shouted Felix.

Suzette began to load the pirogue. She pushed aside a bristly palmetto bush, threw the moss into the pirogue, lost her balance and her footing at the same time.

"O-o-o-o-o-h!" she cried, as she slid into the black, swampy water and floundered about.

Suddenly she heard a hissing and then a grunting sound and, before she knew it, she gave another shriek. Like the surprised squawk of a strange bird, her shrill cry rang through the swamp and sent sharp echoes flying.

Then she saw what it was. There before her, between the pirogue and the shore appeared a large alligator, raising its fearful head out of the water. Crossing the shallow, sluggish stream behind it, other alligators splashed and twisted, churning up foaming ripples. The water, so empty and quiet a moment before, was now alive.

Suzette could not think—but she did not need to.

Marteel, standing on the shore directly behind and above her, held a large armful of moss uplifted, ready to throw. As she heard Suzette's cry, her eyes opened wide with horror. The next instant the moss went flying over Suzette's head and came down with a thud in the alligator's face. The enraged animal let out a thunderous roar.

"Alligator! 'Gator! 'Gator!" yelled Marteel. There was panic in her voice.

"Suzette! My sister, Suzette!" This time there was love and fear.

Then she was in the waist-deep water beside Suzette, pushing and shoving her toward shore.

"Take hold that grape vine," she said, breathless. "Now, up!"

With the help of the dangling vine Suzette climbed up on all fours. Then Marteel clambered up behind her.

" 'Gator! 'Gator!" yelled Marteel again. "Go! Quick!"

The boys did not need to be told. Jacques and Felix were already safely on top of the moss piles in the skiff. They stared at the alligators with frightened eyes. Ambrose jumped in and took the oars.

"Can you bring Suzette in the pirogue?" he cried, looking back.

The two girls were already in.

The alligator, blinded and angered by the moss in its face, was thrashing about wildly in the water, turning and twisting in every direction. The pirogue rocked dangerously up and down on the churning waters.

"You go first, Ambrose," answered Marteel, calmly. "I follow."

She turned once to look back.

"Not Suzette, brother Alligator, not Suzette!" she said under her breath.

CHAPTER FOUR

Hidden Treasure

"YOU HAVE come to the right place, Monsieur!" Papa Jules brought out a chair. "It give me pleasure to speak to you on so engaging a subject. Make yourself comfortable, Monsieur."

As Suzette came into the kitchen, she saw that there was company. Papa Jules was speaking with a strange man, dressed in city clothes.

"You come from New Orleans, Monsieur?" asked Papa Jules, politely.

"My name is Johnson and my home is in Minnesota," said the stranger. "Even as far away as Minnesota, we have heard of the great Lafitte and his treasure. I came to New Orleans for a visit and there I was told to come to Barataria —if I would hear more. I stopped first at the store—Eugène LeBlanc is the storekeeper's name, I believe—and he sent me to you. He said you knew more about the treasure than anybody else."

"Quite right, Monsieur. It is I, Jules Durand, who know more about it than anybody else. Ah, Monsieur, if my brother Moumout had not talked too much, we would be rich today!"

"Rich!" scoffed Maman Clothilde, from her corner by the stove. "If you tell that ole fable 'bout the treasure, don't expect me to sit still and listen." She turned to the stranger. "Digging for treasure, that w'at he like most to do, M'sieu', instead of honest work to support his family."

"There is always enchantment in the search, Madame," replied the stranger, with a smile, "even when you find nothing."

"So I notice, M'sieu'!" said Maman, with bitter sarcasm. "There is all the time more feesh in the sea, even when you ketch not'ing."

Since Maman did not stir to offer hospitality, Papa Jules spoke to Suzette. The coffee pot stood on the back of the stove as usual.

"Bring out cups and pour us black coffee, Suzette," said he. "Monsieur, he drink with me to his new adventure. Ah, if only I were young again, with no care in the world, no wife and no children . . ."

Maman frowned but said nothing.

Ambrose and Jacques stumbled in, followed by Cousin Felix. They were hot and tired after the swamp adventure, but, seeing the stranger, sat down and said nothing. Only Felix, always bold, spoke out.

"Fix me coffee, too, Suzette. I thirsty, me."

Suzette brought coffee. In one hand she held a thin white cup on a saucer. This she handed to the stranger. In the other, she held a cup without a saucer. It had blue and red flowers on it and a gold band round the top.

"Give it to me," demanded Felix. "The swamp, it make me thirsty."

"You can't have my Papa's cup, you." Suzette trembled at his mention of the swamp. She went on talking, to cover his remark. "You might break it. My Papa, he won't drink from no other cup. I give it to him when he sick in bed, that w'y he like it so much. I buy him the nicest cup Père Eugène have in his store."

Papa Jules frowned. He did not like his children to talk so much before a stranger.

Suzette picked up a thick heavy cup with a nick in it, filled it hastily and handed it to Felix. He drained it at a gulp and put it down noisily. "Well," he said, "I gotta go take care of my 'gator eggs, gotta make 'em a nice nest outa straw . . ."

"*Whose* 'gator eggs?" demanded Ambrose. "Them eggs are . . ."

Papa Jules coughed loudly. The boys hushed at once.

"More coffee, Monsieur Johnson, yes? Suzette!"

It was when Suzette came to the stove to pour Mr. Johnson's coffee that Maman first noticed. "W'at I smell?" she cried, sniffing. "It smell like somet'ing dead. It come off you, Suzette."

Papa Jules frowned and coughed, but it did no good. Maman looked at Suzette more closely, then stared. And well she might, for Suzette's dress, only partly dried, was covered with mud and streaked with black swamp muck.

"Where you been, Suzette?" she demanded. "You en't fell . . ."

"More coffee, Suzette!" shouted Papa Jules. "Monsieur Johnson thirsty, him."

Papa Jules was furious with Maman Clothilde. Never had he known her to behave so before a stranger. Such rudeness he would not have. He began to talk loudly, to drown out whatever Maman meant to say next.

All this time Marteel had been sitting on the floor beside the open door. Suzette had brought her inside boldly, but had told her to be ready to leave at any moment. Now Maman threw black looks in the Indian girl's direction. Suzette felt more and more uncomfortable, but she knew Maman could do nothing as long as the stranger was there. She was glad for that, sat down in a chair and rested easier.

" 'Barataria'—a fine word to roll off the tongue, is it not?" Papa Jules was saying. "A town, a bay, two bayous, a light-house and a pass, they all bear the name. The first Jules Durand in Barataria, he got his grant of land from the Spanish king and we be here ever since. My Great-great-grandpère was name' Jules Durand, too, and one hundred year ago, he one of Lafitte's men, him. Ah! The great Lafitte! To have live' in his day—that would have

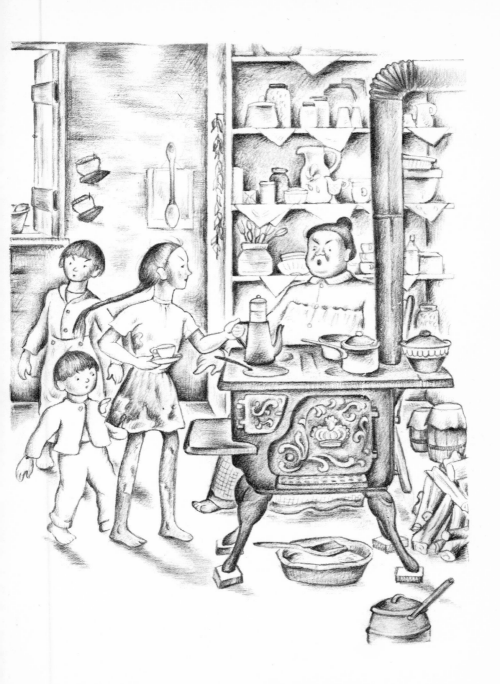

been somet'ing!" In Papa Jules' eyes there came a dreamy look.

"He was a great old pirate, wasn't he?" exclaimed Mr. Johnson, rubbing his hands together. "He robbed the schooners on the sea . . ."

"Pirate?" interrupted Papa Jules, with a frown. "In Barataria, we not call Jean Lafitte a pirate. He a great sea-captain, and the fishermen of Barataria, they sail' his boats for him. They always loyal to their master and when he die, they find his body, they bring it back to the place he love so much and they bury him here. No, we not call Jean Lafitte a pirate. 'Pirate' it not a nice word."

"I agree," said Mr. Johnson. " 'Privateer'—is that better?"

"A great sea-captain, my frien'," insisted Papa Jules. "He object to pay high duties to the government. He wish to correct injustice. He a bold, brave man—all the time courteous and genteel. He knew all the bayous, bays and inlets of Barataria, from the Gulf of Mexico to New Orleans—like a fish know the sea! He knew every island, every Indian mound, every canal, every swamp, every inch of prairie—like a muskrat know its runways!"

Papa Jules tipped back his chair and warmed to his subject.

"Jean Lafitte, he had one hide-out by Grand Terre on the Gulf. He had another right here by the Bayou des Oies —the Bayou of the Geese—and his blacksmith shop too, worked by Negro slaves. His barges, they ran secretly up and down through lake and bayou and canal. He took the smuggled goods to Bayou Coquille—the Bayou of the Shells—then by land to New Orleans and sold them right under the Governor's nose!

"Ah, he one great man, Jean Lafitte!" cried Papa Jules. "You want to see him, my frien'? Every moonlight night he rides his fine white horse 'cross the road by Bayou Coquille—on the stroke of midnight. But it en't him, Monsieur, oh no. It his ghost!"

"You say he is buried in the graveyard here. Is that true?" asked Mr. Johnson, with a smile.

Papa Jules turned to Grandmère. "It true, that, *ma Mère?*"

"It true, M'sieu'," said Grandmère, with quiet dignity. "I have, myself, the honor to take care of his grave. He lies buried in the graveyard by the Bayou des Oies, with all the Durands. Long ago his friends of Barataria, they put up a iron cross over him. They bury him down in the ground, you understand, not on top. It a big hill of shells there, an old Indian mound. My husband's Grandpère, he all the time keep the grave flat. His son and grandson, they do the same. All the Durands, father, son and grandson, they take care of his grave."

The stranger listened to Madame Durand's story politely but impatiently. "There is no doubt that Lafitte had many friends among the fishermen here," he said. "Some

of them must have known where he buried his gold."

"But yes, Monsieur Johnson!" answered Papa Jules, eagerly. "He hide his treasure here. His men, they help him—the great-grandfathers of the men who live here now. Our great-grandfathers, they tell us many places where he bury his gold."

"And you . . . you remember what your great-grandfather told you, Mr. Durand?" The stranger leaned forward eagerly.

Papa Jules nodded his head mysteriously. "My frien' . . ." he began.

"I have a map showing all the bayous, lakes and islands from Lake Salvador to the Gulf," said Mr. Johnson, earnestly. "I have the finest sailing lugger that can be bought and plenty of money to finance the venture. If you will come in with me, I will share the treasure fifty-fifty with you. All you need to do is tell me where to dig—and you will become a rich man!"

"No, Jules, no!" cried Maman Clothilde, panic-stricken.

"No, my son, no!" cried Grandmère, trembling.

The stranger glared angrily at the women. "This is a thing for men to decide between themselves," he said.

"Not too fast, not too fast, my frien'!" said Papa Jules, with a laugh. Then his face turned sober. "There one t'ing I not tole you. When a treasure is buried, a man is killed . . ."

"A man is killed! What for?" cried Mr. Johnson, exasperated.

"So his ghost it guard the treasure, my frien'," answered Papa Jules. "Right in the middle between three live oak trees, that the spot where they bury it. But when once you start to dig, not a word you must speak or the treasure, it sink deep, deep in the earth. So all the legends agree."

"And you believe that nonsense? A sensible man like you?"

Papa Jules shrugged his shoulders. "These fable, they been told by father to son, they been handed down through the generations." He smiled at Mr. Johnson. "They make a pleasant evening's talk, is it not so?"

"Where did you say these three trees are located?" asked Mr. Johnson.

"Ah, Monsieur!" said Papa Jules. "That you must not ask me. If I tell you, the ghost who guard it will spirit the treasure away to a safer hiding place."

" 'The ghost who guard it?' What do you mean?"

Papa Jules turned to Grandmère, who explained. "My husband's Grandpère, he say, when they bury gold, they always kill a man. They cut his neck and put him on top the gold. If you dig, his ghost it come up and watch you. It say, 'You better not dig up all the place, I throw bricks, mud and shells on you.' "

Suzette had heard the story of Lafitte and his buried

treasure many times. She remembered well the time long ago, when Papa Jules and Nonc Moumout and Doreen Dugas' Papa had dug for gold all summer long. But she scarcely listened today, knowing that as soon as the stranger went, she would have the Indian girl's presence to account for. She was trying to think what she would say. She glanced at Marteel, sitting by the open door.

The Indian girl was listening to the treasure story and her eyes were wide and staring. What were they saying, to make her look like that? Suzette turned back to listen.

"So! I understand!" cried Mr. Johnson, rising from his chair, in anger. "I see through you at last! You know where the treasure is hidden, but you won't tell. You've invented this cock-and-bull story about ghosts so you won't have to tell. I see through you! It's not true—there's no ghost at all!"

"But it *is* true, M'sieur!" said Grandmère, emphatically. "Me myself, I have *seen* the ghost."

Marteel's eyes almost popped out of her head, as she stared at Grandmère. Suzette shivered. She was used to talk about ghosts—no one ever took ghosts seriously. But she had never heard so much talk of ghosts as today. Would they never stop?

"You don't want your Indian mounds dug up! You don't want your precious graveyards dug up! So you deliberately invent ghosts to guard them!" shouted Mr. Johnson. "I see through you, I see through your French deceit! Well, you'd better tell, or they *will* be dug up."

Marteel, Ambrose, Jacques and Felix stared, wide-eyed, at the stranger. They had never heard such daring words before.

"Our ancestors, they wish to lie in peace, Monsieur," said Grandmère, calmly. "You would not be so base as to disturb their rest?"

"Have no fear, *ma Mère!*" said Papa Jules. "There are no three oak trees in the proper arrangement in your graveyard."

Mr. Johnson turned to Papa Jules. "Where are they then? Will you tell?"

"Mais non!" said Papa Jules. "Not today, Monsieur."

Papa Jules got up and followed Mr. Johnson to the front gate. From the window, where Maman hastily put her head out, she could see them talking.

It was the first time in twenty-two months that Papa Jules had walked to the front gate, but nobody noticed it. When he returned to the kitchen, everybody was up-set.

"So you go with the stranger to dig treasure, yes?" asked Maman.

"I tole him no," said Papa Jules. "You heard me."

"Me, I can see it in your eye!" Maman Clothilde went on. "You feex to run off and leave us and we never see you again. Me, I hear you tell him you wish you had no wife and no children, you sorry you ever git mar-ried . . ."

"You hear me tell him I not go with him," said Papa Jules, patiently.

The excitement was a good thing for Suzette and also for Marteel. Because of it, the family paid no attention to the Indian girl at all.

Maman and Grandmère threw up their hands and let loose a bursting flood of excited talk, in which ghosts and gold and Papa Jules and men from Minnesota were all mixed up. It took Maman a long time to calm down enough to cook supper and even then the rice was sadly burned.

"Oh, if Jean Lafitte had only died before he was born!" cried Maman. "How much better it be for us all! Oh, if Jean Lafitte would only go back to his grave and stay there!"

Maman had a splendid imagination. She kept expect-ing Papa Jules to dash out at any moment to join the stranger at the gate. All through supper she kept on looking at Papa Jules out of the corner of her eye.

That was how she spied Marteel sitting by the door. She turned on Suzette. "W'at you mean, bringin' that Injun girl back here again? En't I tole you I won't have her round the house? En't I turn her loose? En't I shoo her out?"

"Marteel my frien' now," said Suzette, quietly. "She save me from the big alligator in the cypress swamp."

"Alligator! Cypress swamp! W'at next?" cried Maman, throwing up her hands in great agitation. "First Papa, he go off and leave us, and now, Suzette, she get et up by a ole alligator!"

"Alligator? Cypress swamp?" echoed Grandmère and Papa Jules, and Eulalie who had just come in.

"Who been to the cypress swamp?" demanded Maman, sternly, turning on the children. "En't I tole you never to go there? W'y you not mind w'at I tell you?"

"Ambrose he there . . . and Jacques and Felix . . ." said Suzette.

"Tell us w'at happen, Ambrose," said Papa Jules.

Ambrose told the story. "Marteel, she throw moss in the 'gator's face," he concluded. "She jump in the water and shove Suzette up on the bank, so the 'gator he can't eat her up."

"The 'gator, he twelve feet long," shouted Felix. "I see him good, all the way to his tail."

"Fifteen feet!" "Twenty feet!" shouted Ambrose and Jacques.

The alligator grew longer and longer each moment.

Maman rushed over to Suzette, folded her in her arms, sat down in a rocker and began quietly to weep. "My leetle Suzette! My leetle Suzette!" she sobbed. "To t'ink a wicked ole alligator want to eat her for his ole supper!"

Suzette was no longer a culprit. She had become a heroine.

It was Papa Jules who remembered the Indian girl sitting alone by the door. He turned to Maman Clothilde and said sharply, "Go get your broom, you, and shoo her off. We don't want no dirty Injun round the house."

Maman dried her tears and was thoughtful for a moment. "I can give her a bath, me," she said. "And some supper." The tone of her voice told how sorry she was for the way she had treated the strange girl before.

Marteel ran to Maman and put her arms tight around her neck. Papa Jules chuckled. Suzette took his hand and squeezed it. Maman had come round at last.

That night, a clean Indian girl slept in Suzette's cot with her. She slept with her each night until her new bed was ready. When Suzette showed Maman the bed ticking and mosquito bar she had bought with her money, Maman was pleased. Now that Marteel had saved Suzette's life, of course she had to stay. There was no other way to thank her, and Maman was never one to show ingratitude.

So Maman washed and combed the Indian girl's hair. She threw her dirty rags into the bayou and gave her a hand-me-down dress of Lala's to wear. She even turned up the hem to make it the right length. Maman helped Suzette put the moss to soak and hang it on the fence to dry. After it was properly cured, she stitched up the bed ticking for a mattress and stuffed it. She helped Suzette clear out a corner of the shed by moving traps and nets and poles. They put the mattress on the floor, made it up with the red-checkered quilt and hung the mosquito bar overhead.

And so, at last, Marteel had a bed to sleep in.

CHAPTER FIVE

The New Sister

"MY MAMAN'S got a leetle girl dead."
Suzette and Marteel were walking along the bayou path.

"She got drownded in the by'a," Suzette went on, "when she was four year old. Her real name was Seraphine, but we all the time call her Tit-tit."

Marteel said nothing.

"Right here," continued Suzette, "is where she got drownded."

She walked to the edge of the bank and stood there with her two bare feet placed so that her toes curled over the edge. The embankment went straight down to the lapping water some four feet beneath her.

"Like this," she went on. "Tit-tit was standing here like this. . . ."

A brown hand suddenly clutched her shoulder and pulled her back to the path. "W'at you doin'?" cried Marteel, frowning. "Tryin' to fall in yourself?"

"She fell in flat on her stomach," continued Suzette, unperturbed. "Then a big lugger went by and she got froze and was drownded. My Maman, she cry and cry, and ev'body, they cry and cry. They had a boat funeral —they put Tit-tit in a boat and plenty, plenty people come from the by'a, they all went in boats and they took her to the graveyard on the Indian mound. And now Tit-tit, she dead."

"Dead, yes," repeated Marteel. "Little sister dead. Marteel Suzette's sister now." She smiled her broad, happy smile.

"My new sister," said Suzette, shyly, tucking the Indian girl's arm in her own. "My Maman, she keep little Noonoo, my baby brother, locked up in the yard," she went on. "She not want him to fall in the by'a and get dead."

The two girls strolled slowly on, passing Nonc Moumout's and then Nonc Lodod's house. Suddenly Marteel halted, pointing with her toe to a prickly plant which grew on the slope of the levee. "W'at dat?" she asked.

"Thistle, en't it?" replied Suzette.

"W'at it good for?" asked the Indian girl.

"To prick your bare feets and make you holler!" said Suzette.

Marteel smiled. Using a sharp-pointed branch, she dug the plant up, washed the root off in the bayou, cut open the tender white heart and gave some to Suzette. "It good to eat," she said. "Good for medicine, too. It make a tea, good for the throat."

As they munched the root, the Indian girl looked around.

"If you boil the bark and roots of the live oak tree," she said, "it make a bright red dye to color baskets. Hackberry bark, it make tea for sore throat. Snake grass, that good for snake bite—you chew the leaves and swallow the juice. All the grasses—rat grass, hog grass, pepper grass, broom grass, turkey grass, whooping-cough grass—they all good for somet'ing."

Suzette stared. "How you know so much 'bout trees and grasses?"

"Ole squaw tell me," said Marteel. "She a 'treater'—she treats people. A snake doctor, too—she cure all kind snake bite."

A trio of girls came up the bayou path, arm in arm. They were Beulah Bergeron, Doreen Dugas and Elise Broussard. Elise turned her back at once and gazed across the bayou. The other two looked Marteel over from head to foot.

Then Beulah spoke: "Who dat you got by you?"

"Her name, it Marteel," said Suzette.

"Marteel w'at?"

"Only Marteel, that's all," replied Suzette. "She my frien'. She stay by me, to my house."

This was recommendation enough, but Beulah was still curious.

"She's Injun, en't she?"

"Yes," said Suzette. "She know all about plants and how to make tea out of 'em and make sick people well."

"Me, I went with my Papa to visit the savages once," volunteered Doreen. "We saw baskets, plenty baskets."

"Marteel know how to make bright red dye to color baskets, too," said Suzette.

The girls left off staring.

"We go by Père Eugène, to buy candy balls and sugar hearts," said Beulah. "My Papa, he give me pennies— enough for *her* too. You come with us, yes?"

"Me, I can't," said Suzette, nodding toward Elise Broussard's back. "You know why."

Elise had spoken no word to Suzette, nor Suzette to Elise. The girls passed on. Suzette would have liked to go, but no Durand went anywhere with a Broussard. She gazed longingly after them, thankful they had accepted Marteel so easily.

Suzette looked up at the next house.

"My Tante Céleste, she live here all by herself," she said to Marteel. "She a *vielle fille*—I mean, she got no husband. There she comes now."

Tante Céleste came strolling out toward her front gate. Her sunbonnet was pulled down to shade her eyes.

"Well, if it en't my leetle Susu!" she cried. "And who dat?" She stared at Marteel. "Where she come from? She's Injun, en't she?"

"Yes, Tante Céleste, but . . ." began Suzette.

"Me, I hope them Injuns won't start comin' round sellin' baskets again. They a worse plague than mosquitoes. Send her off."

"*Mais non,* Tante Céleste!" cried Suzette, in distress.

"You en't been to see your Tante Céleste for a long time, Susu," her aunt went on. "W'y en't you? You gittin' proud?"

"Me . . . me . . . I been takin' care o' my Papa," said Suzette.

"W'at! He en't better? He en't worse, no?"

"No. He gone over to M'sieu' Guidry's for a rest," said Suzette.

"A rest from w'at, I'd like to know?" snorted Tante Céleste.

Suzette gave her head a toss. "My Papa, he tired if he want to be, I reckon." She clenched her fists behind her back.

"So that how you take care o' him—lettin' him go 'cross the by'a to gossip with Monsieur Guidry! I see! Who rowed him over?"

"He rowed hisself."

"He *is* better then?"

"He tired, I say," Suzette repeated. "He need a rest. He got pain all the time in his back and he say, it rest him to talk to a frien'."

"Well, it time you come in and pay me a visit," said Tante Céleste. She made her voice sweet again. "I got some frosted *gateaux* just outa the oven. You want to taste one, yes?"

"No, *merci*, Tante Céleste," said Suzette, politely.

But Tante Céleste had her by the hand. In desperation, she reached out the other to Marteel.

"You can't bring no dirty savage in with you," said Tante Céleste, sharply. "She'd track up my floors."

"But, Marteel, she my frien',—she my sister!"

"W'at you talkin' 'bout? You gettin' crazy in the head?" Tante Céleste dragged her unwilling niece in through the gate, closed and locked it behind her. She turned on Marteel. "Go 'long back to the woods, you!

Git 'way from here. Run! Run!"

"Wait!" said Suzette, in a low voice.

The Indian girl nodded.

There was nothing to do but go inside with Tante Céleste. The house was small, but spotlessly clean. The doorstep was scrubbed, the kitchen floor was scrubbed, the kitchen table was scrubbed. Tante Céleste said they were clean enough she could eat honey off any place she chose.

Tante Céleste led Suzette into the parlor and set out a chair. She untied Suzette's sunbonnet, took it off and patted her head. She went to the kitchen, opened her "safe," a neat cupboard painted green, with wire doors, and brought out a plateful of small cakes.

"You like to taste my frosted *gateaux*, yes?"

If anyone else had made them, Suzette would have eaten several with relish. Now she took the smallest one and it was all she could do to choke it down. This she must do for politeness' sake.

When Tante Céleste passed the plate a second time, Suzette shook her head and thanked her coldly.

"W'at a pretty dress you got on!" said Tante Céleste. "But it torn. It must be old. Don't you want me to sew you a new one?"

"No, *merci*," said Suzette. "Me, I like my ole clothes best."

"When you comin' to live with me, Susu?"

"I en't comin', Tante Céleste," said Suzette.

"You en't comin'? W'y not?" asked Tante Céleste.

"How can I leave my Maman? She en't got no leetle girl but me. She need me to . . ."

"Your Maman, she got Eulalie."

"I say, she en't got no *leetle* girl but me. Lala's most grown-up."

"Yes, I hear Lala, she started showin' herself," said Tante Céleste. "I hear Lala, she walkin' out with young Jean Broussard."

"*Mais non!*" cried Suzette, passionately. "She don't like *him*. She *hate* him. It Jean Broussard's Papa w'at shoot our Papa in the back at the shootin' match. En't you remember that, Tante Céleste?"

"Yes, I remember. It en't nice w'at I tell you 'bout Lala," Tante Céleste went on, with a smile, "but it true. I wonder w'at your Papa say when he know."

Suzette turned cold all over.

"It en't true," she said, stubbornly. "My Papa, he won't let Lala speak to Jean Broussard. He won't let eny of us speak to eny Broussard. One time I speak to Elise, Papa he say he gonna whip me if I do it again."

"Well, Lala's most grown-up," said Tante Céleste. "Your Papa, he stay home all the time, but he don't see everyt'ing."

She paused. "You won't come, then?"

"No, *merci,* my Papa, he need me." Suzette hung her

head and said nothing for a long time. Soon a tear rolled
down her cheek.

"I go on with my work then," said Tante Céleste,
"seein' you won't even talk to me."

In one corner of the room stood a four-post bed, so
large that it touched the ceiling. The bed looked strange
now, gaunt and bare, stripped of its usual trappings. Its
shuck mattress, moss mattress, feather bed, feather bol-
ster and pillows, sham straw pillows, mosquito bar, sheets
and quilts made a great mountain, piled up high in another corner.

Tante Céleste brought a pan of ashes, a bucket of water,
a scrubbing brush and cloth. She set vigorously to work.

"The bed, it must be scrub', every inch of it, till it come nice and yellow," she said. "When I get the bed done, I scrub the *armoire,* wardrobe, next. Then I scrub the floor on my knees, till the floor come yalla, yalla, yalla. I won't have no knees left when I git through."

Suzette sat like a lump of wood and said nothing. She wanted to ask, "W'y you all the time scrub?" but she couldn't. The water splashed and the brush moved rhythmically up and down the thick, tall posts.

"You ever hear the story o' this big bed, Susu?" asked Tante Céleste.

Suzette nodded, but Tante Céleste's back was turned. She did not see the nod.

"You never hear 'bout the big hurricane?" went on Tante Céleste. "It was long time ago and my Grandmère —that's your Great-grandmère—was sleepin' in the bed with your Great-grandpère. Nobody come to tell them the storm was comin'—they didn't have eny close neighbors. The wind it start blowin' in the evenin' and kept up all night. They feel the house rock. Grandpère, he got up and went to make coffee in the kitchen. He left Grandmère in the bed. He open the door to look out to see if the storm was gettin' worse, and he let the wind come in.

"The wind, it come in the door and lift the roof right off. It carry it half a mile away in the field. The house, it split in four pieces. Each wall, it fell out flat on the

ground. And there was the bed left right in the middle—
with your poor Great-grandmère in the middle of the
bed. The bed, it hold the house down, Grandpère always
say. If he not make it so big and heavy, the house woulda
blew away, with poor Grandpère and Grandmère inside!
That would have been sad, yes?"

Suzette did not reply.

"My Grandmère," Tante Céleste went on, "she tell me
the hurricane story over and over. When she come to die
—I was leetle like you, then—she say, 'Céleste, *ma cherie,*
I want you to have the big bed, yes. I love you best of all
my grandchildren. I know you take good care of it.' "
Tante Céleste sniffled.

Suzette had never heard this ending to the story. It
was hard to think of Tante Céleste with a Grandmère
who loved her enough to give her a big bed. It threw a
new light on Tante Céleste.

"That w'y you all the time scrub it?" she asked.

"Yes, Susu," said Tante Céleste, still sniffling. "My
Grandmère, she say, 'Scrub it, leetle Céleste, till it come
yalla, yalla, yalla.' So now I do like my Grandmère said,
even if she dead."

It was difficult to imagine Tante Céleste as the obedient
little girl she described, but Suzette did so. She understood better now Tante's passion for keeping everything
so clean, which had made life so trying for other people.
She understood now why she didn't want her floors

tracked up. She was obeying her Grandmère.

"Me, I all the time listen to *my* Grandmère," said Suzette, "and I do w'at she say." She slipped off her chair. "Me, I t'ink I go home now, Tante Céleste."

Tante Céleste wiped her hands on her apron and followed Suzette to the kitchen.

"Please, Tante Céleste, I can have one frosted gateaux, yes?"

The lump was gone now from Suzette's throat. She felt sorry for her aunt, so she asked for a cake. She ate it and thanked Tante Céleste politely. They parted better friends than they had been for a long time.

"I walk to the gate with you, *ma cherie*," said Tante Céleste. She picked up her broom to sweep off the doorstep.

Afterwards, Suzette wished she had not offered to come. They might have stayed friends longer, except for that.

It was when they came round the house that Tante Céleste saw Marteel on the front gallery. Marteel had her feet propped up on a spotless gallery post and she herself lay comfortably stretched out on the spotless gallery floor. Suzette had told her to wait and she waited.

"Look! Look!" cried Tante Céleste, waving her broom in the air. "Look at that leetle savage with her two dirty feetses on the post of my gallery. En't I pound brick dust and scrub 'em till they come yalla? En't I shoo that savage off and tole her to run?"

Marteel calmly put her feet down, jumped off the gallery and stood by Suzette's side. But she did not run.

"Marteel, she my frien'," said Suzette. "Marteel my sister, now."

"Your frien'? Your sister?" cried Tante Céleste. "That dirty leetle savage?"

"Marteel, she clean," said Suzette. "My Maman, she give her a bath."

"Your Maman? A bath?" gasped Tante Céleste.

"Marteel, she live by me, to my house," Suzette went on. "My Maman, she make her a beautiful bed with a mosquito bar. . . ."

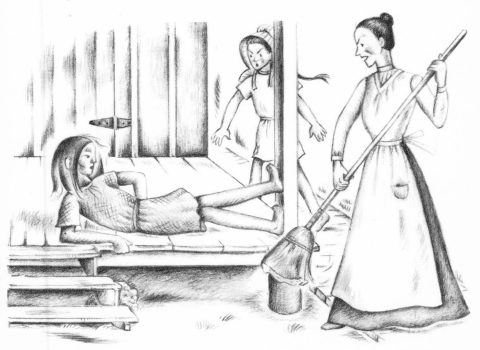

"A mosquito bar?" echoed Tante Céleste.

"And she give her a dress of Lala's to wear," said Suzette.

"A dress of Lala's?"

"And my Papa, he say Marteel, she don't never need to go back to the woods, she got all the time a home with us." Suzette gave her head a haughty toss.

"W'at the matter?" cried Tante Céleste, as soon as she got over her astonishment. "Your Maman and your Papa, have they took leave of their senses?"

"My Grandmère, she say, if Marteel got no family to go to, she can stay by me and be my frien'. Marteel, she my sister now. She listen to my Grandmère and do w'at she say—like me."

"But w'y . . . but w'y . . . your Maman and your Papa and your Grandmère, they do all that?" cried Tante Céleste.

Suzette walked off down the path, her arm round Marteel's waist. She looked back with a smile and replied, "Because Marteel, she save me from the ole alligator who want to eat me up!"

CHAPTER SIX

The Graveyard

"ÉÉ! HÉ! Somebody's cow been here again!" cried Grandmère Durand. "She break down the pickets, she tear down the wire, she trample all over the graves."

"Mebbe the man from Minnesota been here diggin'," suggested Felix. "Mebbe he t'ink Lafitte's gold is buried in the grave with him."

"He won't come in my graveyard," said Grandmère.

Grandmère came to the graveyard every day to clean and keep it in order. Today there was to be a special cleaning and the children, Ambrose, Felix, Jacques, Suzette and Marteel came along to help. They carried a pile of wooden pickets, a roll of wire, several brooms, a hatchet, a bucket of whitewash and a brush.

Felix whispered in Suzette's ear: "This evenin', go home by the big field back of Theo Bergeron's house, where the three oak trees are. Wait under the one nearest the graveyard—you and Marteel, yes. Ambrose and me, we show you big gold pieces."

Grandmère went off with the boys to mend the fence

in the corner. Suzette picked up a broom and handed another to Marteel.

"My Grandpère, he tole me before he die," said Suzette, "the Injuns make this big hill outa shells. I don't know where they got 'em all, me."

Marteel's eyes lighted up. "They eat plenty clams, the Injuns."

"You en't got no Grandmère? No Grandpère?" asked Suzette, sweeping vigorously.

Marteel shook her head.

"No Great-grandmère and no Great-grandpère in the graveyard?"

Marteel shook her head again.

"I sorry for that, me," said Suzette. She leaned on her broom and looked sad. "Then you can't come with us."

"Come with you? Where?" asked Marteel. "Me, I go everywhere."

"Not this time, you can't," said Suzette. "Not on All Saints' Day you can't." She went on to explain. "My Grandmère, she take good care of her graveyard. She get it ready for All Saints' Day."

"W'y she sweep in the graveyard?" asked Marteel.

"She take care of my Grandpère, of course! And my Great-grandpère and my Great-grandmère," explained Suzette. "They sleepin' there in their tombs."

She pointed to the sturdy, well-made brick tombs a short distance away. Grandmère Durand had left the boys fixing the fence and come back. She was hard at work with the brush, whitewashing the first tomb. Up and down she lifted the brush slowly and carefully.

"W'y your Grandmère, she put white on 'em?" asked Marteel.

"For All Saints' Day," explained Suzette. "Each year she paint 'em white. The priest, he come and bless the candles. We put them on the graves of Grandpère and Great-grandpère and Great-grandmère and little Tit-tit. We come at night, plenty people from the by'a, all in a long procession, with candles in our hands. It look purty. The candlelight, it shine on all the painted crosses on the graves. It too bad you can't come, Marteel. It nice, that—to burn candles for the dead."

"W'y I can't come?" asked Marteel.

" 'Cause you en't got no Great-grandpère in the grave-yard, of course!" said Suzette, dropping her broom. "Come, I show you where Tit-tit sleeps."

The graveyard lay on a point of land that jutted out into the bayou at the junction of Bayou des Oies with Bayou Barataria. Formerly it had been a large Indian mound of heaped-up clam shells. The mound itself loomed up, a high hill, in the background. On a lower level space before it were the Durand family tombs, with a flat grave in the center, marked by a hand-wrought iron cross. Farther toward the shore were other graves, some above and some below ground. Some were fenced in, some were

marked by wooden crosses and others by shadow-boxes
in which were placed artificial flowers, saints' statues or
objects connected with the deceased.

Marteel followed Suzette along a narrow path toward
the shore. It was quiet there, with no sound but the lapping
of the bayou waters on the clam-shell beach, several feet
below the steep embankment. They came to a small grave
inside a white picket fence. At its head stood a gabled
shadow-box, about two feet high, with a cross at its peak.
The front was enclosed with glass. Inside, a bunch of

paper roses filled a blue glass vase, and a china-headed doll, dressed in a calico dress, sat staring.

The girls leaned over the low fence and peered through the glass.

"That Tit-tit's doll-baby," explained Suzette, in a whisper. "Before she die, she all the time play with it. Maman, she put it in the grave-box, so Tit-tit won't get lonely, when she sleep in the graveyard."

Marteel's eyes opened wide. "The Injuns, they do the same like that," she said, her eyes glued on the doll. "Me, I not know the white people do it too."

Suzette picked up a big branch which had fallen across the grave. She walked over and threw it into the bayou.

"Suzette! Suzette! *Suzette!*"

It was Grandmère calling. Suzette and Marteel ran quickly back to the Durand tombs. Grandmère looked at them, frowning.

"W'y you drop your broom and leave your work, Suzette? W'at you been doin'?"

"I find a big branch on Tit-tit's grave, yes," answered Suzette. "I throw it in the by'a, me."

Grandmère kept on frowning. Now she was looking at the Indian girl as if she had not noticed her before.

"W'at Marteel want here today with us?" she asked, crossly. "W'y she not stay home and fish? Me, I don't want Injuns comin' in my graveyard."

"She won't hurt not'ing, Grandmère," said Suzette,

picking up the brooms again and handing one to Marteel. "She sweep good. She help me sweep."

"W'at you take her off yonder for?" asked Grandmère.

"She only want to see where Tit-tit sleep," explained Suzette. "I show her."

To Suzette's great surprise, Grandmère reached over and snatched the broom from Marteel's grasp. "Me, I don't want savages sweepin' in my graveyard."

"But Grandmère," protested Suzette, "she sweep good. She won't hurt not'ing. I t'ink, me, you like Marteel, Grandmère."

"Not in my graveyard," repeated Grandmère. She glared at the Indian girl. "You go 'way! Don't come near my graves."

Marteel went obediently off toward the water's edge and sat down. She leaned her back against a tree, listened and watched.

Grandmère went on with her whitewashing. She was working on the second large tomb. Now and then she glanced in Marteel's direction, but seeing the girl sitting quietly, said no more. The boys had finished the work on the fence and gone away.

Suzette worked industriously, sweeping up small branches and the tiny, dead, dry oak leaves which littered the ground.

Grandmère began to speak. "Suzette, I want you to all the time remember this is where Jean Lafitte lies buried." She pointed to the iron cross. "I take care his grave, the same like Grandpère's."

"Yes, I know, me," said Suzette. "I all the time remember."

"On All Saints' Day," Grandmère went on, "the ghost, she come and stay here long time. She pray and she pray and she put candle on Lafitte's grave. She thank me 'count of how good I take care of it."

"You not 'fraid the ghost, Grandmère, when she come?" asked Suzette. "I be 'fraid, me."

"W'y I be 'fraid?" asked Grandmère. "The ghost, she talk nice to me, then she just walk in the by'a, she melt away like swamp fog."

"M'sieu' Lafitte, he bring plenty ghostses!" laughed Suzette. "He bring ghostses to guard his gold pieces, where he bury 'em in the ground, Papa Jules say. You see those ghostses, too, Grandmère? The one M'sieu' Johnson, he don't believe in? The one where Lafitte bury his gold?"

"I don't dig for no gold," said Grandmère. "I let the gold stay where M'sieu' Lafitte he bury it."

"You not 'fraid of the ghostses, Grandmère?"

"No, I not 'fraid of no ghostses." Grandmère sighed.

"W'y you make such a big sigh, Grandmère?" asked Suzette, coming to her side. "You not feel well, no? You been workin' too hard, yes? Let me take the brush, I put the whitewash on for you. I not spill a drop."

Grandmère let Suzette take the brush from her hand

and she sat down on the ground near by. She sighed again heavily.

"You feel tired, Grandmère, yes? You feel sad, yes?" inquired Suzette. She had never seen Grandmère sit down in the graveyard before.

Grandmère leaned her head on her hand. Then she brushed a tear from her eye. "Yes, I feels sad, me. I feels ver', ver' sad."

Suzette put the brush back carefully into the bucket. She came and sat down beside Grandmère. She leaned against her shoulder.

"You mustn't feel sad, Grandmère," she said. "Suzette, she here with you."

Grandmère patted Suzette's hand, then her trouble came out. "When I die, I don't know who gonna take care of my graveyard." Grandmère wept.

Suzette jumped to her feet.

"W'y Grandmère, have you forgot me? Have you not see how nice I put the whitewash on and not make one puddle on the ground? Don't you know I fix to take care of your graveyard after you? Don't you know I all the time listen to my Grandmère and do w'at she say?"

Grandmère looked up and smiled through her tears. "You not 'fraid of ghostses?"

"No!" said Suzette, stoutly. "Of course I en't seen none yet, but when they come, I remem' my Grandmère and I not 'fraid same like my Grandmère."

Grandmère rose slowly to her feet. She put her hands on Suzette's shoulders and spoke solemnly. "You do w'at I say when I gone? You take good care all my graves and Jean Lafitte's grave, the same like I do myself?"

"I promise, me!" said Suzette. "I do w'at you say."

Grandmère wiped her eyes again.

"You not sad eny more, Grandmère, no?" asked Suzette.

"No, I happy now, *ma petite*." She smiled. "I t'ink I go home now for leetle rest. I gettin' old. I let you finish whitewash the big tomb. I come back again 'fore dark, to see how white and purty it look."

Suzette looked anxiously after Grandmère as she walked away, cane in hand. Then she went on with the whitewashing. The tomb was large and it took a long time. After it was all done, she had to go over it again and cover up all the spots and streaks she had missed. Then at last it was done.

The afternoon had passed quickly and dusk was already falling. Dark shadows from the thick-shaded live oaks fell aslant on the Indian mound. Suzette joined Marteel.

"Felix, he waitin' for us," she said. "He gonna dig for gold pieces like the man from Minnesota."

"W'at he want gold pieces for?" asked Marteel.

"Me, I don't know," said Suzette.

Marteel was very quiet and thoughtful. At last she spoke. "W'y your Grandmère not leave the dead people alone? W'y she not make medicine to quiet the spirits of the dead? Then the ghosts not come no more. They sleep in peace."

"Make medicine? W'at dat?" asked Suzette.

"That w'at the Injuns do," explained Marteel. "I see the ole squaw do it once."

"W'at she do?" persisted Suzette. "How she make medicine?"

Marteel broke some branches off a tree and laid them in a circular pattern. "I lay the fire," she said, going through the motions. "I kneel by the fire." She knelt and began to sway back and forth, saying strange words that Suzette could not understand. "I talk to the spirits of the dead. I tell them to lie still. I tell them to stay in their graves and not walk out and make people 'fraid. I tell

them to sleep in peace. When I get done, Suzette, she not
be 'fraid no more." The swaying and strange chanting
continued.

So absorbed had they become, the girls had not heard
footsteps. Suddenly there stood Grandmère beside them.
Her face was black with anger, black as a thunder cloud.

"Wicked savage!" she cried, in a harsh voice. "W'at
you doin'?" She raised her cane as if to strike.

"Oh, Grandmère!" cried Suzette, running to her.
"Marteel, she not hurt anything. Marteel, she tell the

ghostses to lie still and not come out again. She tell them so I won't be 'fraid no more."

"Such heathenish practice in a Christian graveyard!" cried Grandmère, in a shocked voice. "Git outa here, you. Don't you never set foot in my graveyard again!"

"Grandmère! Grandmère!" cried Suzette, weeping. "She only show me how the ole squaw make medicine."

"Chant no good without fire, ole squaw say," added Marteel.

Grandmère looked from one girl to the other. They repeated what they had said and Grandmère listened. Her black looks faded away.

"Don't never do it again," she said to Marteel, seriously. "We not do things like that here. We're not Injuns. We not like it. We do things our own way with our dead."

Marteel nodded as if she understood.

"The whitewash, it purty, Suzette," said Grandmère. "You do it ver' well." Grandmère took up the bucket and brooms and walked out of the graveyard.

The girls followed slowly, letting her go on ahead. Then they cut across to the big field back of Theo Bergeron's house. They saw the three oak trees, went to the one nearest the graveyard and sat down under it. The place was very quiet. The wind rose and the swinging branches made mournful, moaning sounds. Suzette shivered.

"I not like it here, me," she said. "I wonder w'y the

boys not come. Soon it be too dark to dig, yes."

"Mebbe they dig by the light of the moon," suggested Marteel.

"Me, I hope not," said Suzette. "I wish we ask Beulah and Doreen to come and keep us company . . ."

Just then a shower of shells and stones fell from the tree overhead. The girls jumped to their feet.

"W'at dat?" asked Suzette, but Marteel did not answer.

"It . . . it . . ." cried Suzette, turning pale, "it the ghost . . . throwin' t'ings?"

She clutched Marteel by the arm. Marteel showed no fear. Instead, she smiled.

"It . . . it not'ing to laugh at . . ." wailed Suzette.

It was almost dark under the oak tree now.

Suddenly, out from behind the second tree, came a figure in white, advancing slowly. It was dressed in white from head to foot, with no head, arms or legs showing.

"The ghost!" cried Suzette, clutching Marteel. "Tell it to go 'way, Marteel. You not 'fraid of ghostses!"

The white-clad figure moved closer and closer, making a moaning sound that could be clearly heard above the rustling of the trees.

"I . . . am . . . the ghost . . . of Jean Lafitte!" Words now could be distinguished. "Who been stealin' . . . my gold?" A worse shower of mud, moss and shells descended upon the two girls.

Marteel stood still, with a curious smile on her face,

watching the ghost advance.

"Tell it to go 'way," begged Suzette. "You not 'fraid of ghostses."

"I hear you tell Grandmère yourself," said Marteel, "you not 'fraid of no ghostses. You tell the truth?"

"Well, I . . . well, I never see one before!" gasped Suzette.

"You 'fraid?" demanded Marteel. "Remember, I make medicine for you."

"I remember," said Suzette. She remembered, too, how Grandmère was **not afraid** of ghosts.

"No, I not 'fraid," she said, bravely.

"Then do w'at I say," said Marteel, quietly. "Go up to the ghost and pull off his clothes!"

"Oh, I can't!" cried Suzette, wide-eyed.

"Go! Do w'at I say!" ordered Marteel, sternly. "Go! Quick! Do it! Now, this minute!"

Suzette had never heard Marteel speak in such a tone before and she knew she had to obey. She gathered all her courage, rushed up to the ghost and tugged at its white draperies. The ghost did not vanish in the bayou or melt away in swamp fog. It turned to run, but not quickly enough. Marteel was by Suzette's side and together they stripped off the white clothes. The ghost ran, leaving sheet and pillow case in their hands.

It was Felix!

"Ha ha ha! Ho ho ho! You believe in ghostses! You 'fraid of ghostses!" laughed the boys. "You 'fraid of sticks and mud and shells!"

Theo Bergeron and René Dugas and Ambrose and Jacques slipped down from the tree and ran off as fast as they could go.

"Now you 'fraid?" asked Marteel, smiling her broad smile.

"No! Me, I not 'fraid of ghostses no more," said Suzette. "I never be 'fraid of ghostses again!"

CHAPTER SEVEN

A Wild Thing

*J*T WAS true Marteel had a fine bed to sleep in.
But that did not mean that she slept in it.

"Where you sleep last night?" demanded Suzette, when
Marteel appeared on the wharf in mid-morning. "I look
and see—your bed, it en't been slep' in. The quilt, it en't
even muss' up."

"Under the bushes," said Marteel.

Suzette and her father sat on their wharf, baiting a
crab line. Little Noonoo squatted beside them, watching.

"W'y you not sleep in the fine bed I make for you?"
demanded Suzette, severely.

"On the grass, under the bushes, it cool," said Marteel.

"You crazy?" cried Suzette. "It damp out there. It
wet. The water, it never drain off. En't you know, you
get rheumatiz' if you sleep out there?"

"Rheumatiz'?" laughed Marteel. "W'at dat?"

"And the mosquito', they eat you up!"

"Mosquito', w'at dat?" laughed Marteel.

Papa Jules smiled.

"She's a wild thing, don't never forget that!" he said,

in a low voice to Suzette. "No use scolding. You can't tame a wild thing!"

Marteel sat down and helped. Papa Jules cut up the black mullet for bait. Beside him lay a pile of "snoots," pieces of string cut into ten-inch lengths. Marteel's fingers were clever. She tied loops in the ends of the snoots, put the bait in and pulled the loop tight. Then Suzette tied the baited snoots two feet apart onto the long crab line. It would take two hundred baits or more to reach across the bayou.

Felix appeared, his arm full of small sticks of various sizes. He waded at the edge of the bayou, picking and choosing among the drifted branches, sticks and boards which had been washed in against the shore.

"I makin' cages, me!" he announced. "I catchin' blackbirds, me! Gonna eat blackbird stew! You want I ketch you a red bird to put in a cage and hang on your front gallery, Suzette? A pretty red bird, yes?"

Suzette made no reply. Noonoo slipped down off the wharf and began to pick up sticks too, at the water's edge.

Papa Jules frowned and spoke to Felix. "Don't you ever work to help your Papa and your Maman?"

"Me? W'y work?" cried Felix. He went back home, whistling.

Papa Jules shook his head and said, "Brother Serdot, he better look out w'at kind a boy he got."

[91]

"Noonoo, git away from the by'a!" called Maman, from the window. "Susu, don't let Noonoo fall in the by'a. Noonoo, he en't used to the by'a. Suzette, watch him."

Suzette pulled Noonoo safely up to the wharf again.

The baiting of the crab line continued. The sun shone hot and bright.

"Noonoo, git away from the by'a!" called Maman again. "Noonoo! Noonoo! Suzette, where Noonoo?"

Suzette looked around, bewildered. There was Noonoo sitting quietly beside her.

"Here Noonoo, Maman," she cried. "He en't fell in the by'a. He safe by Suzette."

The morning wore on.

Papa Jules finished cutting up the bait and went away. Suzette wondered when the last snoot would be tied. The crab line seemed long enough to reach from Little Village all the way to New Orleans. The sun shone brighter and hotter and the mosquitoes were bad. Now and then Suzette stopped long enough to wave her grass mosquito brush through the air to chase them off.

Suddenly she looked around and saw that Noonoo was gone from her side. "Where Noonoo?" she cried, jumping up.

She looked toward the house, but Maman, fortunately, was not at the pot-shelf window. Suzette's eyes swept the bayou waters on all sides of the wharf. No Noonoo. She ran to the top of the levee and looked over the yard. No Noonoo.

"Where Noonoo?" she cried, in distress. "Marteel, where Noonoo *go*?".

Marteel was still busily tying snoots. At last she looked up. "He carry off sticks," she announced.

"W'y you not stop him?" demanded Suzette, stamping her foot. "W'y you not run after him? W'y you not tell me which way he went?"

Still Marteel went on tying snoots, unconcerned.

Suzette came down and gave her a kick. Marteel could

be very exasperating. "Where Noonoo go, you?"

"That way!" said Marteel, pointing.

"He go after Felix?" asked Suzette.

Marteel nodded.

Like a whirlwind, Suzette set off for Nonc Serdot's house. She must find Noonoo before Maman discovered his absence. She saw Nonc Moumout starting out in his skiff.

"Nonc Moumout, you see Noonoo?" she called.

Nonc Moumout shook his head.

A bicycle bore down swiftly and went whizzing past. Suzette stepped out of its way just in time.

"Jean Broussard, yes!" she cried. "W'y he not look where he goin'? Just like a Broussard, tryin' to kill people, yes!" She made an ugly face at him.

Tante Céleste came out of Nonc Moumout's house. Tante Toinette came out to the gate with her. Tante Toinette was wide and fat and had a mustache on her upper lip. Suzette started to inquire of her two aunts, but changed her mind. It was better they, like Maman, should not know Noonoo was lost.

"Where you runnin' to so fast, *cherie?*" called Tante Céleste. But Suzette did not answer.

By this time she was in Nonc Serdot's yard, with the gate shut tight behind her. She stopped for a moment to catch her breath. There on the front gallery she saw a yellow oriole in a cage.

Suzette walked round the house. Tante Henriette was doing the family wash. She raised her bent back from the tub and put her hand wearily to her head. Suzette's cousins, Odalia and Olivia and Ophelia, were hanging clothes on the line. There were clothes of all sizes, shapes and colors.

"You seen little Noonoo, Tante Henriette?" inquired Suzette, as calmly as she could.

"Seems like he was here a while ago," replied Tante Henriette, in a tired voice.

"You seen little Noonoo, Odalia?" asked Suzette.

"No, I en't!" snapped Odalia. "Me, I been busy washin'."

"You seen little Noonoo, Olivia?"

"No, I been busy washin', too."

"You seen little Noonoo, Ophelia?"

"No, I en't."

It was clear there was no help here. Just then Felix shot out from the back yard like a bullet from a gun.

"Where you goin', Felix?" called Tante Henriette. "Don't go 'way now. It soon be dinner time."

But Felix was already out of sight and hearing.

Suzette hurried to the back part of the yard. The yard was more untidy than others along the bayou. Grass and weeds grew high and uncut, a few fruit trees leaned at crazy angles, while boxes, boards and trash were piled up in odd places. In an old wreck of a skiff, which was falling to pieces, she found little Noonoo. He was seated quietly in a puddle of stagnant water, playing boat with his sticks.

"Oh, Noonoo!" cried Suzette happily, lifting him out.

Her relief was so great, she smiled as Marteel came up, forgetting her former impatience. "There one of Felix' cages," she explained, pointing.

A cage lay near by on the ground. The sticks had been fastened together without nail or string, making a lattice-work contrivance. One side was propped up by means of a stick, with a bait of rice and grits on the ground beneath. When a bird came to eat of the bait, a slight touch of the stick made the cage fall down and hold him captive.

"W'at he catch birds for?" demanded Marteel, with sober face.

"Oh, he like blackbird stew!" answered Suzette.

Marteel frowned. "His Maman, she cook them?"

"Yes," said Suzette. "Blackbird stew, it good."

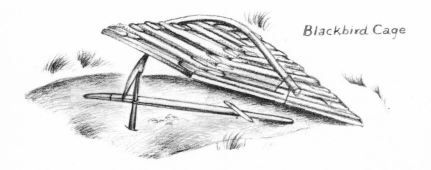

Blackbird Cage

"His Maman, she not have fish enough to eat? Nor rice? Nor beans?"

"Yes, she got plenty fish and rice and beans."

"Then, w'y she eat blackbird? W'at the blackbird do to Felix, he not like them?"

"He like them in stew," repeated Suzette. "Sometime he sell them by Père Eugène. He get 35¢ a dozen for tit-tits, little sparrows, and 50¢ apiece for red birds."

"He *sell* them?" cried Marteel, in a shocked voice. "His Maman let him do that?"

"Yes," said Suzette.

Marteel walked round the yard. She came to a cage in which a blackbird was confined. She lifted it and the bird flew away.

"W'at you doin'?" cried Suzette, in alarm.

Marteel did not reply. She went to several other cages on the ground and she let the birds out. She hunted all through the wilderness of the back yard. She found more cages in the trees and she let all the birds out.

Ophelia peeked through the bushes and cried, "W'at she doin', that Injun girl?" She ran back into the house to tell her mother and sisters what was happening.

"Felix, he gonna be mad when he find out," said Suzette to herself, as she watched.

"The little birds, they my brothers," said Marteel, with a smile. "Now, they not be sold by Père Eugène's store, they not be et in a stew, they not stay all the time in a

cage. Now, they fly in the sky—high, high, like the
clouds. They sing all day, they sing because they happy,
they sing because they free."

"W'at you doin', Noonoo?" asked Suzette. She went
over to a tin tub, which stood beside the old skiff.

"Look!" cried Noonoo, pointing.

"Felix' baby alligators!" exclaimed Suzette.

The bottom of the tub was packed with wet mud, on
which crawled three or four baby alligators, each five or
six inches long, while several others sunned themselves on
a branch of wood sticking out of the mud.

"Remember the eggs the boys got that day in the cypress swamp?" said Suzette. "Felix took 'em away from Ambrose and hatched 'em out."

Marteel took a baby alligator up in her hand. "W'y he not have water in the tub so they can swim?" she asked.

"Too lazy to fill it, or else he forgot," said Suzette. "Looks like the mud's dryin' up, don't it?"

"Yes, they're dyin'," said Marteel, frowning. "They're not lively the way they should be. En't got enough water and en't had enough to eat. Felix ever feed 'em?"

"Some flies now and then when he happen to think about it," said Suzette.

Marteel held out her skirt and put the baby alligators carefully in it, one by one.

When the two girls came round in the front yard again, Marteel stepped lightly up on the gallery and opened the door of the bird cage hanging there. The yellow oriole flew out and away.

"*Mechante gamine!*—you mischievous girl!" shrieked Ophelia, appearing at the open window. "You can't do that, you!" She stamped her foot angrily. "That *my* oriole, you!"

"No more it en't!" said Marteel, calmly.

"W'at you gonna do with the baby alligators?" asked Suzette, when they had closed the gate behind them. Luckily, Ophelia had not seen them.

"Take 'em back to the swamp where they won't die

without water and food," said Marteel, starting off down the bayou path.

Suzette hurried home with little Noonoo. Fortunately Maman had been so busy she had not had time to miss him. Papa Jules came back to the wharf again, with his hunting dogs, Roro and Toto, at his heels.

Suzette was troubled about the birds and the baby alligators, and about what Felix would do when he found out. Felix found out soon enough. It was Ophelia who told him. He came rushing to the wharf.

"Where that Sabine?" he demanded, angrily.

"Gone!" said Suzette, trembling. "Me, I don't know where."

"Wait till I ketch her!" threatened Felix, darkly. Because Papa Jules was there, he said no more.

It was after dark that night when Marteel returned.

Maman scolded her for running away. "You can't have no supper, you. Go on back to the woods."

"Plenty berries, plenty pecan to eat in the woods," said Marteel, but she made no move to go.

The next day Maman's hands were sore. She had used too much lye in the wash water and burned them. Her knuckles were sore, the palms of her hands were sore and she could do no work. But she could still direct others. She set Suzette and Marteel to work to finish sewing the shirts she was making for Papa Jules. They sat on the back doorstep.

Marteel took up the needle and sewed a few stitches. Then she watched Suzette. Suzette repeated Maman's instructions all over again, so Marteel would be sure to understand. Marteel took up her needle again, but she only looked at it.

"The Injun squaws, they don't like to sew," said Marteel. "They like better to make baskets. They take cane and palmetto strips and weave them. They make dyes out of roots, to color them red and yellow and black. They

boil the bark and roots of the live oak tree to make a bright red . . ."

But Suzette was not listening.

"The back-stitch, it hard to make," she said, eyeing her work thoughtfully. "I wonder, me, if I make it right. I go ask Maman, me."

She went indoors to show her seam to Maman. When she came back, Marteel was gone. Her sewing was left lying on the doorstep. Suzette went on with her work, stitching industriously, expecting each moment that Marteel would return.

But Marteel did not come.

Remembering Felix and his threats, Suzette was worried. She picked up Marteel's sewing and took it in the house. When she heard loud voices of children screaming not far away, she hurried off down the path. Soon she joined the crowd.

Felix had Theo Bergeron down on the ground. He was pommeling him hard and calling him a Cajun. Several other boys had Marteel cornered. Ophelia and some of her friends were there too.

Suddenly Ophelia pointed her finger and yelled very loud: "That Injun girl, she turn my yellow oriole loose!"

"She turn all my blackbirds loose!" shouted Felix, jumping up. "She steal all my baby alligators!"

Marteel faced him bravely and said nothing.

Felix marched up close, as if he were going to fight,

but bad as he was, he was not so low as to fight a girl. Instead, he shook his fist under her nose and shouted:

> "Hello, Bean,
> Where you been?
> I been to Bayou Sabine
> To get some haricot bean."

Marteel's face was very sober. She gave one despairing glance at Suzette, then she turned and ran. All the boys joined in a chorus of "Hello-Sabine-where-you-been" and chased Marteel down the bayou path.

Suzette stood still and watched. Marteel was going to the woods again. Each time she went, Suzette never knew whether she would come back again. She hurried home and burst into tears as she told what Felix had done.

"That *petit terrible!*" cried Papa Jules, in anger. "Poor Marteel! She don't like to be called *Sabine* no more than we like to be called *Cajun.*"

"Good riddance!" exclaimed Maman. "Let the little savage go back to the woods. That where she belong."

"You can't tame a wild thing," said Papa Jules. "You can put a wild duck in a cage, but that don't make it tame. You can't change its nature by coopin' it up. Better let her run loose, yes."

"En't I lettin' her run loose?" cried Maman. "En't I let her drop her sewin' on the doorstep and skip right out from under my nose? W'y she not stay in the woods? W'y she all the time comin' round here?"

"For some strange reason she likes it here," said Papa Jules, smiling. "She's starved for a leetle affection, that's all. She en't never had a mother's love."

The next day Marteel was back. She brought two Indian baskets with her. They were very old and were made in intricate design. They were so beautiful Maman could not help but be pleased. She had never seen such fine baskets for sale at Père Eugène's store. She knew he would ask large sums for them if he had them.

Marteel was sorry over running away. She put her arms tight around Maman's neck and kissed her.

"Marteel not Injun no more," she announced. "Marteel white girl now. Suzette's sister, me."

Maman was touched. She could not scold Marteel for running off without showing ingratitude for the baskets.

"W'y you not shoo her away?" asked Papa Jules.

"W'at good it do?" said Maman. "The next minute there she is, back again, with both arms round my neck."

CHAPTER EIGHT

Tit-tit's Doll

THE MINUTE Grandmère came in, everybody knew something was wrong. Grandmère's face was white and her eyes had a frightened look. She was short of breath and sank quickly into a chair.

"W'at the matter, Grandmère?" asked Maman, alarmed. "You walk too fast? You gonna faint?" She turned to Jacques. "Run, get Grandmère a drink of cold water."

Jacques ran out to the rain-water cistern—a large tank behind the kitchen, which drained water from the roof. He unscrewed the faucet and filled a glass with water. Grandmère did not open her eyes until after she had swallowed it.

"Run, Lala, fetch the palmetto fan," said Maman. "Fan her good. She's over-heated. She shouldn't walk all the way to the graveyard in the hot sun."

"W'at is it, Grandmère?" asked Suzette. "The cows, they break down the fence again and walk on your graves? The graves, they been dug up for gold?"

"The graves, they been *robbed?*" cried Maman, imagining the worst. "Are there low-down thieves w'at . . ."

"The man from Minnesota, has he . . ." began Ambrose.

"Be still, all of you!" ordered Papa Jules. "Can't you see you make her worse? Now tell us, *ma Mère*."

Grandmère was silent for a moment, then she spoke. "No! It not the man from Minnesota, but little Tittit . . ."

"W'at!" cried Maman Clothilde, now distracted. "W'at! Somet'ing it happen to my baby?"

"Tit-tit's grave-box . . . it been opened . . . her doll-baby . . . it gone!" Grandmère's words came slowly.

"Oh! Oh! Oh! Oh!" "*Helas! Helas!*" "Robbed! Stolen! Robbed!" Cries and screams filled the air.

Eulalie was washing dishes on the pot-shelf at the open window facing Tante Toinette's. "Tit-tit's grave-box, it been robbed!" she called in excited tones to Tante Toinette.

"*Ma cher!*" cried Tante Toinette. She ran to her window on the other side to tell the news to Tante Thérèse and Tante Thérèse, in like manner, shouted the news to Tante Henriette and she to Tante Céleste. The news spread up and down the bayou through the open windows of the close-set houses.

The whole family was upset and grief-stricken. Anything on hallowed ground was considered sacred. That the doll had been stolen was a shock past believing. Such a thing had never been known to happen before.

The aunts all came running in—Tante Toinette, fat and waddling, Tante Thérèse, neat and stylish-looking, Tante Henriette, untidy and skirts dragging, and Tante Céleste, long arms waving and finger pointing. Nonc Moumout and Nonc Lodod came too. Only Nonc Serdot, away on a fishing trip, was not there. The neighbors appeared and Maman was asked to describe the doll again and again.

"It had a china head with black hair," said Maman. "It had a red and yellow calico dress and two petticoats."

"I know, me!" cried Tante Céleste, eagerly. "It that ole tramp I see round here yesterday. He sleep anywhere, in people's shed, in the ditch, the field. He took it."

"W'at a ole tramp want with a doll-baby?" growled Nonc Moumout. "He spends his time frog-huntin' and snake-huntin'."

"There he goes now—the thief!" cried Tante Céleste, pointing out the door. "Jules, Moumout, Lodod, w'y you not ask him w'at he got in that big bundle?"

The tramp, a forlorn-looking man, whiskered and ragged, was hauled in and questioned. Roro and Toto and even little Poo-poo sniffed at his heels suspiciously. His bundle was opened, but when it was found to contain only a ragged shirt, he was allowed to go on his way.

"It was a beautiful store-bought doll," Maman went on. "Me, I get it by Père Eugène before Papa Jules, he got shot. We had plenty, plenty money then."

"I know! I know!" cried Tante Céleste, excitedly. "You talkin' 'bout brother Jules, how he got shot, it make me remember, that."

She rushed over to her brother. "Jules," said she, "you en't forgot Claude Broussard, no? How you all the time say he your one big enemy?"

All the people crowded close to listen. Interest in the feud between the two families was always keen.

"Eny man w'at shoot me in the back en't no longer my frien'," said Papa Jules, in a loud voice.

"You en't forgot how you don't speak no more to Claude Broussard? And how you won't let your children speak to his children?"

"W'at you drivin' at, Céleste?" broke in Nonc Lodod, angrily. "En't we got trouble enough between the Durands and the Broussards but you gotta hatch up some more?"

Nonc Lodod was dressed in his best store clothes. He had a gold watch in his pocket and a gold chain hung across his vest. He had just returned from New Orleans where he had taken a boat-load of fish, crabs and ducks, which he had sold at a good profit.

Tante Céleste went on mysteriously.

"W'at you say, brother Lodod and brother Jules and brother Moumout, if I tole you w'at I see yesterday? If I tole you I see one Durand and one Broussard walkin' together arm-in-arm down the by'a path and sittin' together on a by'a bench, holdin' hands?"

All the uncles and aunts looked from one to the other, and a murmur of astonishment arose. "Who?" "Where?" "When?"

Suzette had been standing unhappily by, listening. Now she cried out at the top of her voice: "W'at that got to do with Tit-tit's doll-baby?" But nobody listened.

Eulalie turned white as a sheet and leaned against the doorpost for support. Her eyes glanced once toward the outer door as if seeking escape, but she did not move.

"Where you see this, Céleste?" asked Papa Jules, angry now.

"W'at you say, brother Jules," Tante Céleste went on, "if I tole you I see, with my own eyes, one Broussard crawl out from under the graveyard fence, with one bundle hid under her arm?"

"W'at Durand been walkin' out with w'at Broussard?" demanded Papa Jules.

Tante Céleste pointed her finger at Eulalie. "That one!" she said. Everybody looked. "I see Lala holdin' hands with young Jean Broussard on the bayou bench."

"It not true!" cried Suzette, shrilly. "It not true! Lala, she hate 'im, she tell me so!"

But nobody paid any attention to Suzette.

"Eulalie!" said Papa Jules. "It true or not?"

Eulalie nodded her head. "He my frien'," she said, in a voice scarcely above a whisper. Then she lifted her chin and, with true Durand courage, spoke out boldly. "Jean, he not do not'ing. He can't help it, his Papa do the shootin'. Me, I can't help it, my Papa he got shot!"

"Eulalie! Lala, Lala! It en't so, it en't so!" cried Suzette, sobbing as if her heart would break.

Silence filled the room.

Papa Jules sat down in a chair and put his hand to his head. Everybody looked at him and wondered what he was going to do. Eulalie walked out of the room. The people, staring, let her pass. Papa Jules turned to Tante Céleste.

"We gotta find Tit-tit's doll-baby for her," he said. "W'at Broussard you see, with one bundle under her arm?"

"The leetlest one, Ellen Elaine, I t'ink, me," said Tante Céleste.

Felix piped up. "Yes! 'Ellen Elaine, she can't speak plain!' Me, I see her with one big bundle myself."

Nonc Lodod sent Felix to fetch Ellen Elaine at once. She came, a shy little girl of six, and her father with her, Claude Broussard himself. He was a large, heavy man with a round face. Several other Broussards of various ages, including Elise, waited by the gate.

Papa Jules got up to face his enemy. The room grew tense.

"We en't speak together, Monsieur Broussard, for a long time," said Papa Jules. "Today we speak on one important matter. The grave-box of our leetle Seraphine, it been robbed. Her leetle china-headed doll-baby, it been stole out of the box. Somebody here, they see your leetle girl crawl through the graveyard fence with one bundle under her arm."

"W'at o' that?" roared Claude Broussard. "W'at you

make o' that, Monsieur Durand?"

"We want to know one t'ing, Monsieur Broussard," said Papa Jules, calmly. "We want to know w'at was in the bundle."

"Tell him, Ellen Elaine," said Claude Broussard.

"My Maman'th wathing," said Ellen Elaine, lisping. "Me, I took our wathing to ole colored Annie, and next day, me, I go get it." Everybody knew that colored Annie

lived in a shack back of the graveyard and took in washing.

"You see, we en't stole your precious doll-baby, you!" roared Claude Broussard. "You believe me, yes?"

"I not believe one word you say!" shouted Papa Jules. He was angry now. "But I believe your leetle girl, even if she not speak plain. She en't old enough to lie like her father."

"You not believe me, no?" demanded Broussard, again.

"I not believe you when you say you hit closer to the mark, 'cause you lie. You lie, to get one big, fat hog to eat. When you don't get the hog, you come and shoot me in the back."

"So that how you t'ink!" replied Broussard. His voice was quieter now and more earnest. "Mebbe it time for me to set you right about that shootin'. There plenty people here to witness w'at I say it true.

"It was accident. I not mean to shoot. My brother, he come behind me. He pass his gun to me when I not lookin' and it go off when we behind you. That how you got shot. Me, I ver', ver' sorry it happen. I lie awake at night t'inkin' 'bout all the trouble I make. . . ." His big face was red with embarrassment, and he twisted his hat in his hands.

The room was silent with the echo of his words.

Jules Durand said nothing. Broussard took Ellen Elaine by the hand and walked out. The neighbors stepped aside to let them pass. The dogs growled angrily.

"Me, I don't believe you!" shouted Papa Jules, running after Broussard and shaking his fist. "You not sorry, you *want* to shoot me. You want to shoot me, 'cause I better shot than you, 'cause I hit closer to the mark, 'cause I the best shot on the by'a!"

Claude Broussard and his little girl joined the rest of his family at the front gate. He did not answer or look back.

"W'at you mean, lettin' your son Jean, make up to my girl Eulalie?" shouted Papa Jules after him.

But again he got no answer. The Broussards walked slowly up the bayou path and turned in at their own gate.

After a while all the people went away and things quieted down. Suzette brought wood in from the wood-pile and helped Maman start supper. But her head ached with all the tragedy and confusion of the day's happenings. She thought of Eulalie and her story about Jean. She thought of Claude Broussard and his story of the shooting. Her world was suddenly turned upside-down. Was it possible that Papa Jules was wrong? She thought of Ellen Elaine and her story about her Maman's washing—then she remembered the lost doll again.

"That doll-baby, she not walk away by herself, that certain!" said Maman, at the supper table.

Marteel sat silent and ate nothing.

"W'y you not eat, Marteel?" asked Maman.

Everybody looked at Marteel. Then Grandmère remembered the day that Marteel had come to the graveyard with the other children. Grandmère stared at Marteel as if she were seeing her for the first time. Grandmère thought clearly now. Why had she not remembered before?

"Marteel!" she cried, sharply. "W'at you know 'bout this? W'at you know 'bout Tit-tit's doll-baby?"

Marteel shook her head. "Not'ing," she said.

"You sure 'bout that?" questioned Grandmère. "You remember how Suzette, she show you Tit-tit's grave? You remember the grave-box with flowers in it and a doll-baby behind the glass?"

"Yes," said Marteel.

"You en't steal it, Marteel?"

Marteel shook her head.

"She's lyin'," whispered Grandmère to Maman. "I can tell. She took it, I'm sure, me."

"Oh, oh, oh, oh!" cried Maman. "W'at you mean, Suzette, takin' that savage into the graveyard? Don't you know Injuns can't never be trusted? Don't you know they take everyt'ing they see? 'Cause they all the time t'ink it belong to them? Don't you know not'ing en't safe with an Injun around?"

"But Marteel, she en't never touch' not'ing! She en't never took not'ing. W'at you scoldin' her for? She en't steal the doll-baby," wailed Suzette.

"We soon see about that," said Grandmère, with determination.

Grandmère walked straight out to the shed, to Marteel's beautiful bed. Marteel and the family followed. The moss mattress lay on the floor, the coverings were mussed and tumbled, the mosquito bar had fallen and was tangled up with the bed-clothes.

"Marteel, w'y en't you make your bed up neat, like I learn you?" scolded Maman.

Suzette held her breath.

Grandmère pulled the mosquito bar and covers off to one side. She lifted the moss mattress—and there, on the floor beneath, lay Tit-tit's lost doll. It lay neatly arranged in a little curled-up nest of Spanish moss.

Marteel said nothing. She did not speak when she saw Grandmère's accusing eyes on her. She did not speak when she saw Grandmère pick up the doll and when she heard Maman's loud lamentations. She looked from one to the other, confused.

Suzette took Marteel by the hand. Her heart began to pound in her breast, but somehow, she knew Marteel was innocent. She would trust her first, until everything was explained.

"W'at you mean, stealin' Tit-tit's doll-baby?" Grandmère turned angrily on Marteel, took her by the arm and shook her. "You wicked thief!"

"Me not thief!" said Marteel, stubbornly. "White girl, me. Suzette's sister, me."

"See w'at happen for lettin' her stay?" cried Maman. "She t'ink she one of us, and w'at we have is hers. Injuns en't got no moral sense. They take w'at they lay their hands on."

"Suzette's sister, me," repeated Marteel. She pointed to the doll in Grandmère's hand. "Suzette's sister's doll-baby . . . Marteel's doll-baby now."

"See! Hear w'at she say!" shrieked Maman. "She say

the doll-baby hers, yes! She call it hers, yes!"

"She t'ink . . . she t'ink . . ." said Suzette, trying to explain, "she taken Tit-tit's place . . . she really my sister and so . . ."

"Nonsense! Injun blood is Injun blood!" cried Maman. "She en't no more your sister than a rabbit. Me, I put up with enough from her and it the last straw, this."

Papa Jules turned to Maman. "I hear you say she got

herself wrap round your heart? W'at kinda mother is
that, to turn her loose?"

"She en't not'ing to me," protested Maman, frowning.
"Just an orphan savage Suzette picked up. I en't her
mother."

"Your heart, it en't big enough to take in an orphan
child, I reckon," said Papa Jules, in a low voice.

"She en't not'ing to me, I tell you," repeated Maman.
"She gotta go."

"You right, Clothilde," said Grandmère, sternly. "We not keep her round here after this, no. Nobody know w'at she do next. Nobody know w'at goin' on inside that head of hers."

"She gotta go," cried Maman, "and this time never come back."

Papa Jules said no more.

Grandmère set her lips in a firm line. "Marteel," she said, "we tried to make you welcome here, yes. But it a dreadful t'ing, this—takin' the doll-baby. It so dreadful, we can't have you round here no more. Go back to the woods to your own people and stay there."

"Oh, Papa Jules!" cried Suzette. "Don't let her go! Don't! Don't!"

"Go on, you! Git outa here!" ordered Maman, pushing Marteel along.

The Indian girl raised her arms once as if to put them round Maman's neck. Then she dropped them limply at her side, seeing it was no use.

Suzette knew that Maman meant it this time. Suzette saw the sadness in Marteel's eyes. She saw her walk slowly toward the gate, her shoulders hunched. There was no use appealing to Papa Jules. Like Maman and Grandmère, he wanted Marteel to go, too. Suzette threw herself down on the moss mattress and sobbed bitterly.

"W'y you all hate her so?" she wailed. "W'y you make

her go 'way again? She en't done not'ing. Marteel, my sister, my sister!"

Grandmère carried the doll carefully back into the house. With loud exclamations and noisy talk, Maman and the boys followed.

It was quiet in the yard after they left. Papa Jules came to the shed and touched Suzette on the shoulder. She went with him to the front gate. Marteel was not yet out of sight. Together they watched her leave the bayou path and turn into the woods, without looking back.

Papa Jules took Suzette by the hand and her tears stopped coming.

"The Injuns really believe that," he said. "They believe that when one person dies, another can come and take his place. Marteel was only carrying out an old tribal custom. She thought she was taking Tit-tit's place and so Tit-tit's doll rightfully belonged to her. Taking it was not stealing. Taking it was not doing wrong. Poor Marteel, she'll find it hard to be a white girl, yes. Mebbe she better off with her own people."

"That w'y you let her go, Papa?" asked Suzette.

"Yes, that w'y I let her go."

CHAPTER NINE

A Christmas Guest

ALL SAINTS' Day, November first, came and went. The china-headed doll was replaced in Tit-tit's grave-box and the glass was carefully sealed. The usual candle-blessing ceremony was held, when the people of the bayou went to the graveyard and prayed for the dead.

It made Suzette very sad. It made her remember how she had forbidden Marteel to come because she had no ancestors there. Marteel had not come, for she was gone, gone, perhaps for good. Suzette held her candle and made her prayers by Grandpère's grave and by Tit-tit's grave. Then she made another prayer. She prayed that Marteel might come back.

Soon the winter trapping season opened and most of the neighbors left for a three months' stay in the prairies. They packed bedding, provisions, furniture and trapping supplies, and removed, with their families, to the marshy trapping grounds, to spend the winter trapping muskrats. It was the only way to make money in the winter time, and one by one, they went sailing off in their luggers down the bayou.

Two of Nonc Lodod's finest luggers went past the house, sailing abreast, towing his fine new house-boat behind. The phonograph was playing a merry tune and Tante Thérèse waved her arm from the lace-curtained window.

"If only we had a house-boat!" cried Maman. "If only Jules had any kinda boat of his own!" The tears rolled down her cheeks. "Jules, he never make no money, him," she said, sadly. "He too lazy to go trappin'! He want to loaf round all the time and do not'ing. Each time he went trappin' before he got shot, he come back with not enough money to pay for w'at we eat while we gone. He never have none left over. We never get no silk dresses, no nice shiny shoes, no phonygraph to make music."

Suzette put her arms round Maman's waist. "W'at matter dat?" she said, bravely. "Me, I don't want no silk dress, no shiny shoes, no phonygraph."

"Better times, they come," said Grandmère, "if only you hold up your chin. Jules, he get stronger and next year he go trappin' and get rich, mebbe."

"Mebbe," repeated Maman, bitterly.

"W'y you not go trappin' muskrat in the prairie?" she demanded, when Papa Jules came in. "Your brothers they go, the neighbors they go, ev'body go but you."

"Can't *swim* to the trappin' grounds," said Papa Jules. "Can't go trappin' without boat and supplies. And my back, where the bullet is, it get stiff and sore, when I go in damp, wet place like the prairie."

"Plenty excuse!" sniffed Maman. "That bullet in your back, it not'ing but rheumatiz."

Papa Jules shrugged his shoulders, picked up his gun and whistled for his dogs. "Me, I fish crab, I fish fish—when they bite—and when they don't, I go huntin'. Make two-three cent today, we eat tomorrow."

"For months now, you en't make half a dollar," said Maman.

But all the scolding did no good. Papa Jules continued in his lazy ways, absent more and more often from home, hunting, thus, however, keeping the family well supplied with game.

Days passed. One morning the faucet on the rain-water cistern was frozen and had to be thawed out.

"Cold weather it bring *le jour de Noël!*" cried Maman, smiling.

"Our Maman, she won't let us forget Christmas, no?" said Papa Jules, with a laugh. "It good, that. *La Christine,* our Santa Claus, must git a hearty welcome. All we need is plenty money to spend!"

"Plenty money!" sniffed Maman. "W'at you t'ink? You so lazy, mebbe we git two-three cent to spend for Christmas."

Papa Jules said nothing. He only smiled.

"Nonc Lodod and Nonc Moumout and ev'body come home from the trappin' grounds," cried Suzette, happily.

It would be wonderful to have Beulah and Doreen and all their neighbors back, though only for a few days. Suzette's eyes brightened as she thought of *le jour de Noël* and counted the days. Then her face fell. If only Marteel would come! She wanted no presents for herself. She wanted only Marteel.

The day before Christmas, Papa Jules came into the kitchen laden down with mysterious packages and on top of them, two fat ducks. Maman eyed him suspiciously, so he explained.

"Me, I killed a big buck and Eugène, he shipped it to market and give me a good price for it."

"How much?" demanded Maman.

"Oh, two-three cent!" laughed Papa. Everybody else laughed too. "Now, en't you glad I go huntin' every day? En't you glad that big buck make Christmas for us? Oh yes, here two fat ducks I brought down—cook 'em for dinner tomorrow."

The mysterious packages disappeared from sight. Maman forgot all her worries and set to work. She loved to cook and Christmas dinner was worthy of her best efforts. There was chicken and oyster gumbo, fluffy white rice, roast duck, white cream tarts and a layer cake. Tante Toinette and Nonc Moumout came to help eat it, drink wine and enjoy the fun.

The meal had hardly begun when little Noonoo came running in. "A big new lugger with a red sail!" he shouted, pointing out the front door.

"Now who comin'," cried Maman, "just when we ready to sit down!"

Papa Jules hurried out to find the lugger already moored to the end of his wharf. The children followed at his heels.

"Good day, sir!" said an immaculate gentleman, stepping ashore. He stretched out his hand.

"Monsieur Johnson!" cried Papa Jules, delighted, taking the hand in both his own. "From Minnesota! My good frien', how fine to see you again. And just in time for Christmas dinner. Where you been so long?"

"Lost!" replied Mr. Johnson. "I expected to be back in Minnesota in time for Christmas, but I got lost in those confounded marshes. My maps are no good. They show only about one-quarter of the waterways. I never knew what a labyrinth Louisiana is! You go down one stream or bayou or coulée, only to find yourself in another. I've been going round in circles for days!"

"How you find yourself again?" asked Papa Jules.

"One day, in a deserted spot, I ran across an Indian girl who spoke good English and she directed me to Bayou Barataria. Then I knew where I was."

An Indian girl! Suzette's heart missed a beat. But the men went on talking and she had no chance to ask questions.

"Come in! Come in, take Christmas dinner with us!"

cried Papa Jules, bubbling over with hospitality.

"But it will be troublesome for your wife . . ."

"Not at all! Not at all!" cried Papa Jules. "She t'ink it an honor to serve you her roast duck."

Mr. Johnson could not refuse the cordial invitation, after his dreary days on the bayous. The visit was a gay and happy one. After dinner, Mr. Johnson told of his gold-digging adventures. He told of visiting all the places where Jean Lafitte was said to have buried his treasure. He told of exploring Barataria Bay, Grand Isle, Grand Terre and many adjacent islands and shores.

"And w'at you find, my frien'?" asked Papa Jules, with a sparkle in his eye.

"Nothing! Not a single gold-piece for all my pains!" answered Mr. Johnson, laughing.

"Then you not rich, M'sieu'?" asked Maman, wide-eyed.

"Poorer than when I started," replied Mr. Johnson, "for I've spent all my money."

"It good, that!" murmured Maman.

"You mean, good that I am poor again?" exclaimed Mr. Johnson.

"Oh no, M'sieu'," cried Maman, in great confusion. "I only mean, it good . . . that Jules, my husban' . . . he not go with you!"

"So it goes! So it all the time goes, yes!" cried Papa Jules. "Many men, they been fools before. They have risked much and lost everyt'ing. But w'at a fine fable, is it not? And w'at a great man—Jean Lafitte! Always the French fishermen of Barataria, they will do him great honor."

"And digging for gold," added Mr. Johnson, "is the greatest sport of all."

Suddenly a loud knock came at the door. Suzette opened it, giggling, and a strange, half-grown figure stepped in, dressed in a long, loose, woman's wrapper. His cheeks were bright red, smeared over with elderberry

juice, and he wore a crown of Spanish moss wrapped round his head. He carried a long switch in his hand and a loaded burlap sack over his shoulder.

"Here comes *La Christine!*" he announced. "Any good children here? Any bad children?"

Joseph and Jacques stepped boldly forward. "We good! We good!" they cried, eagerly.

"No, you bad, and I switch you!" *La Christine* chased them round the room.

Noonoo, frightened, ran and hid behind Maman's chair. *La Christine* approached quietly, looking in all directions. "Any good leetle boy here, name' Noonoo?"

"Here! I . . . me good!" cried Noonoo, peeping out.

"I got somet'ing for you," said *La Christine,* " 'count of you been such a good boy."

He opened his big sack and took out a little red wagon for Noonoo. Then he gave a monkey-on-a-stick to Joseph, a tea-set to Suzette, a base-ball bat to Jacques and a bottle of perfume to Eulalie. Last of all he brought out firecrackers, which all the boys pounced upon and which were soon set off to a noisy popping.

Papa Jules turned to Mr. Johnson. "It not Christmas in Louisiana without firecrackers."

"It sounds more like Fourth of July to me," said Mr. Johnson, laughing.

During the excitement, *La Christine's* wreath and wrapper fell off, and there was Ambrose, red-faced and

[129]

merry, in the midst of the fun.

There were no gifts for the elders—no phonograph, no silk dresses, no shiny new shoes—but no one mentioned the fact.

At last it was time for Mr. Johnson to go. The family all went out to the wharf to watch his departure. Mr. Johnson thanked his friends for the happy Christmas, shook hands all round and stepped aboard the lugger. He put his head inside the cabin and spoke to a passenger there: "I thought you were going ashore here. Isn't this where you wanted me to bring you?"

A small dark-skinned figure, with tangled hair and ragged clothes, came out of the cabin and stepped from the lugger to the wharf. She moved forward confidently, never once doubting her welcome.

"That's the girl who guided me back to civilization," said Mr. Johnson, as the boat shoved off.

"Marteel!" cried Suzette. She ran to her side and took her hand. "You come back for Christmas?" she whispered.

Marteel nodded, smiling. "Christmas—w'at dat?"

No one else spoke. Mr. Johnson's lugger moved slowly out into the bayou, while the family watched. When it had passed round the bend, Marteel ran to Maman and reached up her arms. But the look on Maman's face made her drop them again.

"W'at you come back for?" inquired Maman, coldly.

"En't I tole you to go back to the woods and stay there?"

"White girl, me," said Marteel. "Suzette's sister, me."

"There she goes again . . ." began Maman.

"It Christmas, Clothilde!" said Papa Jules, gently. "En't your heart big enough?"

"Have you forgot w'y we shoo her off?" demanded Maman.

Grandmère had been watching the look on Suzette's face. "We can't shoo her off on Christmas, Clothilde," she said, softly. "And look how dirty she is . . ."

"W'at she needs is a kind Maman to give her a bath," added Papa Jules. "A kind Maman . . ."

Suddenly a loud squawking was heard coming from back of the house.

"Run, Suzette, see w'at that is," cried Maman. "Somet'ing been killin' my hens. Bring in the eggs while you there. I make omelette for supper."

Suzette darted over the levee and into the yard. Marteel looked at Maman's face again and then, without a word, followed Suzette.

That summer, several rows of okra had been planted down the length of the garden. Their prickly dead stalks reached from the shed to the picket fence which separated the yard from the marshy field beyond. Suzette saw the squawking hen between the rows and chased her.

Suddenly she stopped short in the path. "O-o-o-o-h!" she screamed.

There at the end of the row stood a wild-cat, ready to pounce on the hen. "Ee-ee-ee-ee-ee!" hissed the animal.

The hen got away and came toward her. Suzette stood staring. Her breath was gone. She couldn't scream now.

"Run back!" The sharp words hit her ear. A hand touched hers and Marteel was beside her.

Suzette looked down in the path in front of her. The wild-cat was there now. She saw Marteel's bare, brown foot on the struggling animal's head. On the fence beyond, she saw three more wild-cats with angry eyes, hissing mouths and spreading whiskers.

"I hold him. You run!" Marteel's words came again.

Then Suzette saw the animals on the fence leap down upon the hen in the path and roll over fighting. The air was filled with flying feathers, but there was no more squawking. She screamed and ran.

The screams brought Papa Jules and Ambrose, with their guns, running. The screams brought the dogs, Roro and Toto and little Poo-poo, barking. Bam! Bam! Bam! Bam! The shots followed one after the other in rapid succession. The wild-cats turned and fled, with the dogs at their heels.

Afterwards, no one knew exactly how many wild-cats there had been, but one thing was sure. At least two of them would never leap the fence again.

Marteel sauntered slowly toward the house, where the family waited by the back doorstep.

She looked up at Maman with a glint in her eye. "That hen, she won't never lay no more eggs," she announced.

Maman said nothing. She turned to Suzette and listened as she began to tell about Marteel's bare foot on the wild-cat's head.

Suddenly Maman took the Indian girl in her arms, held her tight and wept. "And I tole you to go back to the woods!" she wailed. "Marteel! My leetle Marteel!"

Papa Jules looked on, surprised.

Maman tried to explain: "She en't not'ing to me—but she's got herself wrapped round my heart and me, I can't turn her loose."

"*Joyeux Noël!*" said Grandmère, softly, "Merry Christmas!"

CHAPTER TEN

Mardi Gras

"I threw a stick up in the plum tree,
Some oranges they dropped down—
Oh, let me poom-ta-la-le
Oh, let me go play! go play!

They fell kerplop upon my head,
Broke two of my toes right off—
Oh, let me poom-ta-la-le
Oh, let me go play! go play!"

"Y YOU sing?" asked Marteel.

"'Cause I happy!" said Suzette, softly.
"Spring it here."

The girls came round toward the front of the faded
orange-colored house. A flash of red caught Suzette's eye.
A cardinal sat on a branch of the blossoming peach tree,
whistling a gay tune. In the corner by the fence, the little fig tree was leafing out, and beneath the bedroom window, the rose-bush was in full bloom.

"Grandmère, she plant the rose-bush when she came,
a bride, long ago to live in this house," Suzette explained.
"She gave it to me to take care of." Pulling a half-opened

bud, she tucked it behind the Indian girl's ear. "Now you look purty, Marteel."

Marteel pulled another and tucked it behind Suzette's ear. "Suzette purty, too," she said.

Inside the house, Maman took up the song Suzette had begun. The window was open, to let the spring sunshine in, and they could hear her voice plainly:

> "I am going out to plow
> Where there is no land at all—
> Oh, let me poom-ta-la-le
> Oh, let me go play! go play!
>
> I put my horse upon my back
> I put my plow into my pocket—
> Oh, let me poom-ta-la-le
> Oh, let me go play! go play!"

"W'y she sing?" asked Marteel.

"She happy, too," said Suzette. "Spring it here, I tole you!"

"W'y ev'body happy in spring?"

Suzette thought for a moment, then replied: "In spring comes Mardi Gras." She ran lightly up on the front gallery. Then she pointed to the *parterre*, the narrow, fenced-in flower bed beside the steps.

"Me, I gonna buy flower seeds by Père Eugène," she said. "Pretty four-o'clocks I plant here, to bloom all summer."

"W'at for?" asked Marteel.

"To look purty, of course," answered Suzette.

"Plenty flowers in the fields and woods," said Marteel.

"Each day," said Suzette, "when the four-o'clocks open up, it time to go in and drink coffee! You wait here, I ask Maman 'bout Mardi Gras." She went indoors and Marteel listened.

"W'at! Masks and costumes?" cried Maman, amazed. "W'at you t'ink? When Papa he owe Père Eugène money for all the flour and sugar we eat all winter? No, Père Eugène, he mad at your Papa. He won't give you not'ing for Mardi Gras."

Suzette came back and sat on the step beside Marteel. "Maman say, we can't have no Mardi Gras. Me, I don't care, but w'at I gonna say to Beulah and Doreen?"

Marteel did not appear to be listening. Suzette took her by the arm and shook her. "W'at I gonna tell them?"

"Mardi Gras, w'at dat?" asked Marteel, with a grin.

Suzette explained that soon Mardi Gras or Fat Tuesday would come, a day to be joyfully celebrated before the beginning of Lent. Like all the bayou children, Suzette looked forward to it with longing.

Marteel shrugged her shoulders, got up and walked off down the bayou path. Then she began to run and finally disappeared in the woods. All the rest of the day she was gone. Late in the evening she returned, saying nothing.

On Mardi Gras morning, Beulah and Doreen came early. Suzette hid in the shed, unwilling to face them, but

Marteel dragged her out. Marteel's eyes shone bright and she behaved mysteriously. "Come," she said. Suzette came and Beulah and Doreen followed. As they went along, they were joined by Felix, Ophelia, Theo and Jacques.

"Come with me," cried the Indian girl, and they all followed her to the edge of the woods.

"Mischief afoot!" exclaimed Tante Céleste, sourly, standing by the gate.

"On Mardi Gras," laughed Maman, "w'at else you expect? Père Eugène he won't give no mask for the children to have a leetle fun. Marteel she smart girl, she fix somet'ing."

Soon the excitement began. Young children appeared with stockings or paper bags, in which holes for eyes and nose had been cut, drawn down over their faces. Others had their faces blacked with soot or wore store-bought masks and costumes. An older boy who looked suspiciously like Ambrose was dressed in a woman's long skirts and sunbonnet. He carried a willow switch and chased the children, shouting:

> "Mardi Gras, chick-a-la-pie,
> Run away and tell a lie!"

Then suddenly, back from the woods, came the others, dressed in outlandish Indian costumes, with duck and goose feathers stuck in their hair and bright stains, red, yellow and black, painted on their faces. It looked as if

Marteel had not only raided the Indians' wardrobes but the old Indian squaw's dye-pots as well.

"Mardi Gras, chick-a-la-pie,
Run away and tell a lie!"

Up and down the bayou path the children shouted and war-whooped, brandishing long willow switches and shaking noisy gourd rattles. The smaller youngsters were soon chased and frightened into their homes, but bravely peered out the windows. In everything, Marteel was the leader. It was she who invented the strange sounds the whooping troop made, the strange steps they took, the strange antics they played. She seemed like a different creature, come from some gayer, brighter world, to bring new life to this.

"That Sabine!" scowled Tante Céleste. "Bringin' all them savage clothes and feathers and dances right here to the by'a! It en't Christian, that!"

Papa Jules tweaked her ear. "Go paint your face and put on a fancy dress and mebbe somebody'll kiss you, Céleste!"

"Don't forget, it Mardi Gras!" cried Maman. "Marteel, she give the children more fun than they ever had before, bless 'er heart."

The fun reached its height that night in a Mardi Gras ball held in the whitewashed hall next to Eugene LaBlanc's store. The village musicians—Arsene Cheramie with his fiddle and Alcide Brunet with his accordion—furnished the music, while young and old danced to their rollicking

tunes. All the men were masked and disguised in loud-colored, fantastic clothes. Nonc Moumout wore deer antlers on his head, his face was blacked and he roared like an alligator. Many of the women were dressed in old-fashioned dresses taken from attic trunks. The smallest children were left on benches along the walls, and babies were put to sleep on the floor beneath, to allow their gay mamans to join in the fun.

Suzette and Marteel skipped happily about among the crowd. They discovered Eulalie dancing with a young man wearing a clown mask and suit, and followed the couple till they came to rest on a bench. Suzette crept behind them, curious. She reached up suddenly, lifted the white mask from the youth's face and saw that it was Jean Broussard.

"*Ma foi!*" she exclaimed.

"Git outa here, you leetle Sabine!" he shouted gaily.

Lala and Jean together—should she tell Papa Jules? How furious he would be! But it didn't seem dreadful now. It was all part of the fun. Before she could do anything about it, the couple went flying off, hand in hand.

Refreshments were sold at the rear of the building—gumbo, cocoanut and pecan pralines, anise-seed cakes, lemonade and black coffee. Suzette watched Lala and Jean settle down to enjoy huge dishes of gumbo and rice.

"Buy us some gumbo," she begged, coming up. "Marteel and me hungry too."

The young people went on eating and paid no attention.

"I hear somebody say it time for the men to unmask!" cried Suzette. But Lala kept on talking to the clown as if she did not hear.

"Papa Jules, he comes!" shouted Suzette. "You better run, Lala!"

This time Lala heard. "Where, Susu?" she cried.

"There!" cried Suzette, laughing. "He got Maman's sunbonnet on his head and rabbit gloves on his hands — and oh, see his ruffled apron!"

Eulalie and Jean waited to hear no more, but skipped out the open door and away. After they left, the fun reached its height, when all the men pulled off their masks. Then the jollity stopped at midnight sharp, because no one would think of dancing on Ash Wednesday.

So the day came to an end, as even the happiest days always do, and Marteel, the sprightly Sabine, shed her cloak of gaiety. The next morning she went off to the woods again, returning the clothes she had borrowed. After that she did little work and seemed lazier than ever, as if all her energy were spent.

Easter came early that year, and preparations for Easter meant housecleaning. The weather continued bright and sunny and soon Little Village was in a great upheaval.

Joseph and Jacques sat on the front steps, hammers in hand, pounding fragments of red bricks into dust.

"W'y everybody scrub?" asked Marteel. Such excessive

cleanliness seemed entirely unnecessary to the Indian girl.

"Ev'body gotta get his house clean for Easter," explained Suzette.

She brought a bucket of water and set it on the front gallery. She sprinkled powdered brick dust over the floor, then took her broom and began to scrub. Marteel leaned against the gallery wall at the other end and watched idly.

"You gotta all the time keep your house clean," Suzette went on. "Every morning, Maman she dust and sweep. Once a week, she scrub with a brush."

"W'at she do dat for?" asked Marteel.

"That good cleanin', Maman say," replied Suzette. She

swished the water over the floor in great puddles. "Me, I like better scrubbing with a broom. When you scrub with a brush, it wear out your knees, it hurt' your stomach and it git your arms all tired. I git tired quick, me."

"W'y you do it then?" asked Marteel.

" 'Cause my Maman, she tell me to, of course," said Suzette. "Git outa my way or I drown you!" She tipped the water in Marteel's direction, which made her move leisurely down to the bottom step.

Maman came round the house with her arms full. She carried two brooms, a bucket, a brush on a long pole and a rake. She walked round the front gallery and disappeared on the other side.

"W'at her walkin' round the house for?" asked Marteel.

"She gonna sweep down the outside walls. The house gotta be clean on the outside, too. She gonna rake up the leaves in the yard. She gonna scrub the board walk to the shed," explained Suzette. "Plenty work to do, you lazy t'ing. W'y you not help?"

"W'at for?" asked Marteel.

"Look, see all the other women working," said Suzette, pointing. The same things were happening at all the other bayou houses. Suzette lowered her voice to a whisper. "All the women do it," she said. "You gotta do it too, or they talk about you."

Suzette finished her scrubbing and put broom and bucket away. After the floor was dry, she brought an arm-

ful of winter clothing and hung it out to sun on the clothes-
line, stretched across the gallery. Then she sat down on the
step beside Marteel to rest.

Beulah Bergeron and Doreen Dugas came walking by.
They stopped to talk.

"Oh, Susu!" cried Beulah. "My new hat, it got pink
roses on it."

"Me, I gonna get my hair curled," said Doreen. "My
Maman, she gonna put it up in curl papers."

"My new dress," Beulah went on, "it got lace and in-
sertion all over the ruffles, and my new shoes, they patent
leather."

"My dress, it got blue polka dots," said Doreen, "and a
wide blue sash. And I got new slippers with silver buckles."

Suzette did not speak.

"W'at you got for Easter, Susu?" asked Beulah.

Suzette gave her head a defiant toss. "My Maman, she
got more important t'ing to do than fuss makin' new
dresses," she said.

"Marteel, she en't got one neither?" asked Doreen.

"No," said Suzette.

The two girls walked on.

"W'at dat they talk about?" asked Marteel.

"Their new Easter outfit," said Suzette.

"W'at dat?" asked Marteel.

"You hear 'em," said Suzette, with impatience. "New
hat, new dress, new sash, new shoes, new everyt'ing—all

w'at they gonna wear for Easter."

"You wear 'em too?" asked Marteel.

"No," said Suzette. "Me, I like my ole clothes best."

"W'at they wear shoes for?" asked Marteel.

"Stop askin' questions!" scolded Suzette, sharply. She heard voices inside the house now.

Maman had not used her brooms and buckets and brushes after all. She was in the kitchen, talking to Papa Jules and Grandmère. With all the doors and windows open, they could be heard plainly.

"Me, I go 'cross the by'a," said Papa Jules, loudly. "Guidry, he give me a job on his plantation. I plow sugar cane for a change. He tole me he give me work any time I ask for it."

"*Mais non!*" cried Maman, alarmed. "You can't never work the land. You not a farmer. You a fisherman."

"Mebbe I not a fisherman, after all," said Papa Jules, with sadness in his voice.

"All the Durands, since the first one came from France, they been fishermen," said Grandmère. "They have love' the sea and the bayous of Louisiana. They go to sea and come back with the t'ings of the sea, to feed and clothe and shelter them and their families. You got the sea in your blood, my son. You can't run away from it."

"The sea, it wicked! The sea, it treacherous!" shouted Papa Jules, angrily. "Sometime it give, sometime it take. All the time, it try to break a man's body . . . and his spirit, too. That the truth and you know it."

"*Mais non,* my son!" said Grandmère, quietly. "All good t'ings, they come from the sea."

"How 'bout storms and hurricanes and floods?" demanded Papa Jules. "You call them good?"

"Your Père and your Grandpère and your Great-grandpère, they never worry about food or shipwreck or storm," said Grandmère, "they love the sea so much. When a storm come, the fisherman, he wait patiently for it to pass, and always, it pass."

"The life of a fisherman, it not'ing but a gamble," said Papa Jules, bitterly. "Riches on the one hand, danger and death on the other."

"All life, it a gamble," said Grandmère, "but when you show courage, the rewards are worth the struggle."

"How can I be a fisherman," shouted Papa Jules, "when I not got even a boat of my own?"

Maman spoke up. "W'at matter dat? We get along somehow. You en't never had a boat, and we en't starve' yet. Not with the by'a full o' fish at our doorstep, we won't."

"I go 'cross the by'a," said Papa Jules again. "I go see Guidry."

"Yes, Jules," said Maman, quietly. "A good t'ing to try, that."

Suzette heard her father's chair scrape on the floor, as he rose to his feet. She heard his footsteps on the board walk as he came round the house. She watched him get in the skiff and go.

Monsieur Guidry was as good as his word, being short of help. So each day Papa Jules rowed across the bayou, coming home at night. For this reason, it was Ambrose who started the early gardening. He dug a "canal" or narrow ditch round the four sides of the garden patch to drain off the water. After the soil dried out, he spaded and hoed it fine. On Holy Thursday he made high ridges the length of the patch, ready for planting.

On Good Friday it rained, but Maman planted her beans anyway. She made holes in the top of the ridges with her hands and dropped the beans in. It was muddy work, for no tools might be used on Good Friday. It rained hard for the rest of the day. The family took only bread and coffee without milk, as it was a time for fasting. That night they waited till long past bedtime for Papa Jules, but he did not come. They went to bed and in the morning learned that he had not come home at all.

Still it rained, pouring heavily all day Saturday.

Grandmère and Maman and the children sat sadly in-doors. All the wooden shutters were tightly closed, and a lamp burned with a flickering yellow light above the kitchen table.

Once Joseph and little Noonoo begged to go out to pick white clover to make nests for the Easter rabbit. "Me, I go too," said Suzette.

"You want to go out and drown, yes?" asked Maman.

They opened the window and looked out. The canal round the garden patch had overflowed into the paths between the rows. The bean rows were already covered.

Then they heard Papa Jules coming. His rubber boots splashed through the flooded yard.

"Next time I come home," he announced, laughing, "I row the skiff right over the levee and tie it up by the kitchen door!" He never guessed how true he spoke.

Everybody laughed. It was good to see him again.

"If the water get higher," he explained, soberly, "Guidry, he lose all his sugar cane. Me, I gotta go right back. We do w'at we can to save it. We work all night, mebbe."

He ate his supper hastily.

"The rain, won't it never stop?" cried Maman, in despair. "Beans planted on Good Friday make the best crop, but . . . ours, they all wash' away."

"Beans, they easy to plant again," said Grandmère.

"If it not stop soon," said Papa Jules, trying to joke, "me, I go to the Indian mound and build us a palmetto hut on the very top! Then we keep dry all right!"

Once again, he knew not how true he spoke.

CHAPTER ELEVEN

High Water

"THE CREVASSE is come! The crevasse is come! Ev'body gotta run away!"

It was Easter morning. Suzette rubbed her eyes and jumped quickly out of bed. She could not believe the words she heard. She knew all too well that a break in the Mississippi River levee was called a crevasse.

"Oh, my three purty orange trees! Just when they all nice in blossom, they gonna get drown'." That was Tante Céleste.

"Moumout, he gone to get palmetto leaves. . . . He gonna start buildin' on the Indian mound. . . ." That was Tante Toinette, breathless.

"Lodod, he say we go up to New Orleans, we not stay here." Tante Thérèse spoke up.

"Maman . . . Maman . . ." Joseph and Noonoo began to cry.

Suzette dressed quickly and hurried out to the kitchen. The aunts were there all talking at once. The room was nearly dark with windows and doors closed. A coal-oil lamp burned dimly on the wall. Suzette pushed one window shutter partly open and looked out. She shut it again quickly, as if anxious to blot out what she had seen. She looked around, saw that Eulalie and the boys were all up and dressed, but the Indian girl was not there.

"Where Marteel?" she asked.

Nobody answered her question. She stared at her aunts in the dim half-light. Their hair was uncombed and they were only half dressed, with shawls thrown over their shoulders.

" 'Tit Pierre and Gros Paul, they bring word," Tante Thérèse went on, " 'bout the crevasse and tell ev'body to run away quick!"

"W'at we gonna do?" wailed Maman. "Jules, he en't slep' home for two night . . ."

Little Noonoo and Joseph began crying more loudly.

"On Easter, too!" cried Tante Céleste. "Me, I put my new outfit on that Lodod got for me . . ." Her flowered lawn dress looked sadly out of place. Already the bottom ruffles were soaked with muddy water.

"Go take it off again!" said Grandmère, sharply. "Nobody gonna wear a new outfit today." Grandmère was burning palm leaves before the Virgin's statue on the shelf.

"The Mississippi can't never hold all that water," Tante Thérèse continued. "The levee got to break somewhere."

"The giant river, he got many mouths, but he all the time try to find a new one," said Tante Toinette.

"And we all get drownded like muskrats!" moaned Tante Céleste.

"Nonsense!" said Grandmère. "There been crevasses before, and there be crevasses again. Anybody who lives in the bayou country knows that. Only make up your mind w'at you gonna do, that's all."

"My three orange trees . . ." began Tante Céleste again.

[153]

"Go, get a spade and a box," ordered Grandmère. "Dig 'em up, plant 'em in the box and put the box up on the roof of your shed. Then mebbe you can save 'em."

"But me, I can't lift 'em up . . . ." Tante Céleste began.

"Go, do w'at I say," said Grandmère. "Then move all the furniture you can up to the attic. You be surprised w'at you can lift at a time like this."

Tante Céleste opened the door, lifted her ruffled skirts high and splashed out.

"Don't waste so much time talkin'," said Grandmère to the other aunts. "Go home, move your furniture up—the t'ings you want most to save."

"Where's Marteel?" asked Suzette again.

"Don't ask me," said Maman. "I en't seen her."

"Did she come in from the shed?" asked Suzette.

"Me, I don't know," said Grandmère. She turned to the aunts. "Go home, do w'at I say and do it quick!" she ordered.

They pulled their shawls up over their heads and splashed out.

Suzette remembered that she had not seen Marteel for a long time. She threw on a shawl and went out. It was still raining heavily. When the door was opened, a flood of water came pouring in over the kitchen floor. The yard was now covered to that level. The doorsteps were entirely covered. Only the top half of the picket fence could be seen.

Suzette waded through the water to reach the shed, but Marteel was not there. Her bed, which had not been slept in recently, was floating. Suzette remembered now that Marteel had helped Ambrose spade the garden on Thursday, but she had not seen her since. On the way back to the house, she rescued some struggling chickens from the water and set them on the roof of the chicken house. Just as she returned to the back door, Papa Jules appeared in his skiff. He rowed it over the low levee, in through the front gate and tied it up by the kitchen door, just as he said he would. But he was not joking now.

"Oh, Jules, Jules!" cried Maman, falling into his arms. "It true, yes? It a flood, yes?"

"Yes," said Papa Jules, "but not'ing to get excited about. A crevasse in the Mississippi. High water it coming, but coming slow. The break, it seven mile from here—so we got plenty time. Too bad Guidry had to lose all that sugar cane. We built a levee round the field and kept pilin' dirt higher and higher, but we can't keep the water out. So he say let it go and sent us home to look after our families. Me, I come soon as I could."

"W'at we do? W'at we do?" wailed Maman.

"Take the furniture up to the *grenier*," said Grandmère, sternly.

"Yes, that the first t'ing," said Papa Jules.

"Where Marteel?" asked Suzette. "She can help."

But no one knew or had time to think of the Indian girl's

absence. The boys helped carry things out on the front gallery and lift them up the steep ladder-like stair. Suzette and Eulalie helped Maman take the dishes off the shelves and pile them, with the groceries, in baskets.

When she could find nothing to do, Suzette opened the front bedroom window and looked out. Water covered all the floors now, so she crouched on a chair. The anxiety about Marteel faded, as other worries crowded close.

Her flower seeds in the *parterre* by the front gallery were all washed away. She need not look to see. The little stunted fig tree in the corner by the fence was standing deep in water. She remembered how each winter it got frozen back and had to start growing all over again. Now it had big green leaves—would it ever bear fruit? She looked down at the rose-bush, just beneath the window. It was still blooming bravely with most of its branches under water. Each year, all summer long, there were roses to pick. Grandmère gave the bush to her to take care of . . .

She jumped up suddenly and rushed toward the back kitchen door.

"Where you goin', Susu?" asked Grandmère.

"Me, I gonna dig up the rose-bush, and lift it on top the shed, like you tell Tante Céleste 'bout her orange trees."

Grandmère shook her head. "Water too deep, *ma petite*," she said, gently. "Too late now. Better let the rose-bush go."

Suzette went back to her chair by the open window. The

tears rolled down her cheek one by one.

Papa Jules took a heavy load up to the attic and then came down again. He stopped in the bedroom.

"W'at you cryin' for, Susu?" he asked, harshly.

"My four-o'clocks . . . me, I bought seed by Père Eugène and now they all . . . wash' away!" she wailed.

"Flowers, bah!" scolded Papa, angrily. "Seeds—they easy to plant again. W'y you not cry for the sugar cane that bring money for food for you to eat and clothes for you to wear?" Papa Jules went out the back door, got in his skiff and rowed away.

"Don't cry, *ma petite*," said Grandmère. "You feel bad 'bout the rose-bush, but cryin' won't help any. It only make Papa Jules cross to see you cry."

Suzette could not leave her place by the window. The water kept on rising inch by inch. The whole yard looked like one enormous lake now, stretching across the bayou and off in all directions. The wharves had disappeared from sight, and crab-cars, boxes, pirogues, barrels, branches and trash floated in all directions.

"W'at a mercy the water it come up slowly," said Grandmère. "It give time to make our plans."

Papa Jules came back with Nonc Moumout in his lugger. The two men poled it round the house, then, with the help of the boys, loaded cow, pigs and chickens on board. Papa Jules came into the house for a moment. The first thing he saw was Suzette crying at the bedroom window.

"W'at you cryin' for, Susu?" he asked again.

Suzette stammered. "For . . . my rose-bush!" She hid her face in her hands.

"For your rose-bush? W'y you not cry for the lost sugar cane? For the money your Papa not earn?"

Papa Jules stamped out of the room angrily. In the kitchen he spoke to Maman. "Me, I take the animals to the Indian mound. I stay and build us a palmetto hut to camp

in. Can't tell how soon I come back."

"Oh Jules, you go off and leave us?" cried Maman. "With the water still rising?"

"There en't no other way," said Papa Jules. "Gotta fix a dry place for us to stay. The high water, it don't go down for months when it come from a crevasse in the levee. Don't stay below here too long and get sick. Go upstairs, wait in the attic. Where Marteel? Seen her?"

"Gone again," said Maman. "Always gone when we need her most."

"She not drownded, no?" asked Suzette, anxiously.

Papa Jules shook his head. "Me, I come back for you soon as I can. Be ready to go."

Suzette watched the lugger, with the stock aboard, pull out of the yard and sweep slowly round the house. Then Maman said it was time to go upstairs. They all climbed up and changed to dry clothes.

The attic bedroom, with its low, sloping roof, was dark and overcrowded now with all the furniture. A window with a shutter opened out at the south gable end. Suzette took her place beside it and looked down over the yard. She could still see the fig tree's green leaves and the rosebush's pink blooms.

Maman and Eulalie and Grandmère bustled around, sorting and arranging furniture, clothing and supplies, to have everything in readiness when Papa Jules came to take them away. But he did not come till the next day. The first thing he saw was Suzette still crying.

"W'at you cryin' for now?" he demanded.

"For . . . for the sugar cane!" she stammered. But in her heart, she knew it was not true.

The men brought the lugger up close to the front gallery and loaded on bedding and supplies. Maman and Eulalie and the boys climbed down the ladder and went aboard.

"Who next?" called Papa Jules, loudly.

"Nobody," called Grandmère.

"You not comin'?" asked Papa Jules, surprised. "And where Susu? She not here."

"We stay here," called Grandmère. "Suzette, she stayin' by me to keep me company."

"W'at this?" growled Papa Jules. He came up to the attic and scolded angrily.

"Me, I come here fifty year ago when Grandpère bring me a bride," said Grandmère with a smile. "I been here ever since and I en't never gonna leave. If the house go in the high water, me, I go with it. It my house and I love it."

Suzette put her arms tight round Grandmère's waist.

"You won't come then?" asked Papa Jules.

"Me, I stay here," said Grandmère.

"Me, I stay by Grandmère," said Suzette.

Moumout was shouting below for Jules to come. He could not argue longer. He turned to Suzette. "You stop cryin' if you stay by Grandmere?"

"Yes," said Suzette.

Papa Jules kissed them both and went down the ladder.

The next day Suzette sat by the window again and watched the high water swallow up first each pink rose on the rose-bush, then each green leaf of the fig tree. After the rose-bush was gone, she had no interest in anything. She saw boats pass the house loaded with people, animals and furniture. She saw roofs of houses carried by on the swollen bayou, she saw dead snakes, birds and alligators float past. But for all these things she had not a single tear. Somehow she did not care.

The days passed one by one. The rain stopped but the water kept on rising.

Suzette felt sick. Her head ached and her body was hot from head to foot. Grandmère prepared food as well as she could without fire, but Suzette would not eat. She lay all day on a moss mattress without speaking.

Nonc Serdot and Nonc Moumout came to try to take Grandmère away, but succeeded no better than Jules. Grandmère refused to leave.

Then the ladder itself was submerged and the lake outside the window was almost up to the sill. Days passed and the two, marooned in the attic, were left alone. No one came to see them. Although Suzette ate almost nothing, the food supply dwindled and Grandmère grew silent and thoughtful.

At last the water reached its peak and began to drop gradually. One day they noticed it had sunk a full foot

beneath the sill. When a large, **heavy** plank came floating past the window, Grandmère reached out with a broom and drew it up against the house.

"W'at dat for?" asked Suzette.

"I go get somet'ing, me," said Grandmère.

Without another word, Grandmère stepped out onto the plank and, using her broom for a paddle, began to pole the plank upstream. So many strange things had happened —this was only one more.

[162]

"Where you goin', Grandmère?" asked Suzette, as she watched the swaying plank rise and fall on the water.

Grandmère did not say, but promised to be back soon.

Grandmère came back, not poling the plank, but seated in a pirogue, with Marteel at the paddle.

"Me, I bring you a doctor," said Grandmère.

Suzette smiled. It was good to see Marteel again.

"Me, I go to the palmetto huts at the Indian mound," Grandmère went on, "but nobody got medicine. It all been left in the houses and wash' away in the flood. Me, I feel ver' sad, I don't know w'at to do . . . no doctor, no medicine. Then Marteel, she come in one of them Indian's pirogues. I tell her how sick you be, so she pick Spanish moss and boil up some tea for you over Maman's fire."

Marteel let Suzette look in the basket she brought. It contained a little pile of black cured moss, a few roots and herbs, bits of deerskin, and a large bottle filled with a dark brown liquid.

"Me, I be a 'treater' like the old squaw," said Marteel.

She poured some of the liquid into a cup and handed it to Suzette. She leaned over Suzette's bed and swayed her body back and forth, while she mumbled Indian chants and memory prayers. Suzette thought of the ghost chant in the graveyard long ago and Grandmère's black anger. But now, Grandmère looked on approvingly, so she lifted the cup and drank.

The next day Marteel came again and brought a brew

made from the bark of the hackberry tree for Suzette's sore throat, and after that, she came each day for a visit. Grandmère, hopeful now, gave Suzette frequent doses of the strange-tasting medicines. Soon Suzette began to grow better and was ready to eat again. And Marteel earned Grandmère's lasting gratitude.

One day Marteel worked busily as she sat by Suzette's bed. Toward evening, she handed Suzette a strange-looking doll, whose body, arms, legs and two pig-tails were made of braided Spanish moss. It had tiny shining sea-shell eyes, deerskin shoes and apron, and a string of beads about its neck. Suzette laughed, it was so funny.

"An Injun doll? A leetle Sabine?" she asked.

Marteel nodded and a broad grin spread over her face. She took from her basket some flat, shiny, pointed discs and fastened them to the doll's dress. "Wampum!" she explained. "Dyed scales from the gar-fish, they make good wampum, yes?"

Suzette nodded. "You ketch gar-fish?"

"No," said Marteel. "Sabine Joe ketch 'em. I get the scales by him."

"Sabine Joe? Who dat?"

"Just a ole no-count Injun," said Marteel, shrugging her shoulders. "His mother, she the ole squaw." Marteel frowned.

"She hurt you again?" asked Suzette.

"No!" Marteel showed her white teeth in a quick laugh.

"She too old, can't catch me no more. Me, I run away quick."

"Where you stay when the levee break and high water come?"

"On the big high Injun mound called 'the Temple'— where Bayou Perot meet Bayou Rigolettes," said Marteel. "All the Injuns come, they eat and sleep there. Plenty animal come too—deer, muskrat, coon, opossum, rabbit, skunk, all kind."

"You keep dry?"

Marteel nodded.

CHAPTER TWELVE

The Indian Mound

"GRANDMÈRE, come look!" called Suzette.
Grandmère stepped out on the gallery.

"Company come!" cried Suzette, pointing. "Remember you hear a rooster crow in front of the house this morning? That a sure sign and here come the company."

"Ugh!" cried Grandmère. "Me, I don't like that kind o' company. Go 'way, you."

A ten-foot alligator lifted its nose up the front steps and opened its toothy jaws to let out a roar. Then it swung across the yard making deep tracks in the soft mud.

"Too bad Papa Jules, he en't here," said Suzette. "Then Mister Alligator wouldn't be so nosey."

"Too bad Marteel en't here," said Grandmère, smiling, "so she could jump on his back and take a ride."

They both laughed as they watched the animal waddle awkwardly up and down over the levee and plunge into the bayou waters. After he disappeared, Grandmère and Suzette walked over the yard. The little fig tree in the corner by the fence was dead and so was the rose-bush under the window. They looked at them sadly, but said nothing. Then they went back into the house.

"Mud, mud everywhere," cried Grandmère, "outside and in. All the house, it not'ing but mud. W'at you poor Maman gonna say when she see it!"

"We clean it up," said Suzette, practically. "Me, I go back with Ambrose and bring Marteel to help."

Suzette was well again, but she and Grandmère were still living in the attic bedroom. Day by day the waters had receded and finally, in late June, the bayou had resumed its natural level. Ambrose came daily in the skiff, bringing food cooked by Maman on the Indian mound

The next day Suzette went back with him.

As they moved along, she looked and saw the bayou front sadly changed. Wharves and boat-houses were badly wrecked or washed away. Debris was piled up everywhere —boards, boxes, uprooted trees, trash and dead animals. A heavy coating of slimy, muddy ooze covered everything.

"Tante Céleste's orange trees they died, even up on top of the shed," said Ambrose. "Nonc Lodod and Tante Thérèse never went to New Orleans at all. Their house-boat and lugger both got wrecked when an uprooted tree crashed into 'em."

"Oh!" cried Suzette. "Such a purty house-boat, too. Where they go?"

"They stay by us at the mound," said Ambrose.

"Tante Thérèse in a palmetto hut?" cried Suzette.

"Yes," said Ambrose, with a smile, "and she don't like it much. Some people had to live in trees till boats came and took 'em away to New Orleans or Grand Isle or other places. A man told Papa his leetle boy died and he put him in a wooden box and put it up between the branches of a big tree—till the waters went down, so he could bury him."

"Oh dear!" said Suzette.

She stepped from the skiff and ran up the steep shell bank, where, on the opposite side of the mound from the graveyard, the palmetto huts stood. Maman, Eulalie and the boys, and all the aunts came running to greet her and tell her how well she looked. Then she hurried over to see Maman's hut.

Like the others, it stood upon stilt legs, high off the slope. It had two wide bunks built against the back wall, one above the other. The floor was piled high with boxes and baskets of clothing and supplies. In one corner stood Tittit's grave-box, safe and dry.

Suzette sat down on a log in front of the hut to talk to Maman. Joseph and little Noonoo played with some boats which Ambrose had whittled out for them.

"Some days we had only dry bread to eat," said Maman, "when the water came up to the hut floor. But we kept dry and the Red Cross relief boat brought us rations of grits and salt meat and cane syrup. After the shells dried off, we made our fire on the ground and cooked again." She pointed to the camp-fire, where bread in a Dutch oven, covered over with hot coals and ashes, was baking. "Good t'ing I remember to bring Grandmère's yeast!"

The cow put her head round the side of the hut and mooed contentedly. Clucking hens scratched for bugs among the clam shells. The pigs rooted noisily near by.

"No grass here," said Suzette. "You had enough to feed the cow?"

"Plenty," said Maman. "The boys, they pull leaves and moss off the oak trees—she like it, yes."

"And the pigs?" asked Suzette. "W'at you feed 'em when you en't got no corn or potatoes?" Suzette opened her eyes wide. The pigs, tiny before, were so enormous now, she scarcely recognized them.

"We feed the ole sow plenty alligator meat," explained Maman. "She give plenty milk and fatten the pigs quick."

"Alligator meat!" exclaimed Suzette.

"And the chickens!" Maman threw up her hands. "They lay so many eggs, we never eat 'em all, we had to give 'em away."

"W'y they lay so many eggs in a flood?" asked Suzette.

"Alligator meat!" answered Maman, laughing. "W'at we do without them ole alligator, me, I don't know. *Le bon Dieu*, the good God, musta sent 'em to take care of us . . ."

"Where you get so many alligator?" asked Suzette. "Marteel, she bring 'em from the Injuns?"

"En't you hear? En't nobody tole you?" cried Maman. "W'y Papa Jules and Nonc Moumout and Nonc Lodod and the boys, they go 'gator huntin' eny time day or night and get a skiff load. The flood, it wash all the alligator outa the swamp and bring 'em down 'long the by'a. When the water it high, we see 'em all round the mound, lookin' at us. Ugh! I not like it, me."

"W'at they do with so many alligator," asked Suzette, "after the pigs and chickens is fed?"

"They melt the alligator grease, just like a pig, and Papa, he sell the oil," explained Maman. "Papa he sell the teethses, he get a dollar and a half a dozen for the big ones to make rings for babies to bite on and bracelet for ladies to wear and frames for people's spectacles. And then all the hides! The hide-buyer, he give good price for 'em."

"Where Papa now?" asked Suzette. "Me, I wanna see him."

"Huntin'," said Maman. "He happy when he go huntin' every day. But me, I sick o' cookin' on the ground like a savage, I sick o' skinnin' alligator. Me, I wanna go back home again."

"The house, it deep in mud," said Suzette. "Grandmère and me, we went inside and looked."

"Mud or no mud, me, I wanna get back home again," sighed Maman.

Suzette looked around. It did look like an Indian camp. No wonder Maman was not happy.

"Where Marteel?" she asked. "She en't been to see me for a long time, she en't."

"There!" exclaimed Maman, pointing. "All the time off somewhere. This wild way of livin' just suits her—*la petite sauvage!*"

Suzette looked down to see Marteel in the pirogue round the bend in the bayou below. Marteel waved and motioned for her to come.

"She callin' me," said Suzette. "I go for leetle ride."

"Mind you not let a ole alligator upset you," warned Maman.

Soon Suzette was sitting in the bow of the pirogue,

which moved leisurely along under the Indian girl's sure hand. She waved to Maman on shore. It was pleasant to be with Marteel again. The sun shone with the welcome warmth of summer time and it was almost possible to forget there had ever been a flood. Soon they came into the smaller Bayou des Oies.

"They call this the Bayou of the Geese," said Suzette, " 'count of all the ducks and geese that feed on plants and seeds here."

The girls watched ducks come winging down and settle on the water, their ki-ki-ki sounding louder as they came closer.

"No geese now," said Suzette. "Only wood ducks and black ducks stay through summer."

"The wood duck," said Marteel, pointing, "it the purtiest duck of all—with its red eye and bright-colored crest. The Injuns, they used to take its neck feathers and put 'em on their calumets—pipes of peace."

The pirogue slid over the quiet waters while Marteel talked softly to the ducks. Several of them had alighted on the branch of an overhanging tree. Now and then they cried a shrill hoo-eek as if in answer to the Indian girl.

"Old Canada goose, he come back in the fall," said Marteel, softly. "When the north wind begin to blow in late summer, he start off for the southland. He stop here and rest, eat seeds and grow fat again. Then he get up and go— he don't set down on the ponds no more. He fly far, far across the Gulf before he light down again."

"When we look up," said Suzette, "and see so many geese pass, we say 'plenty cold this winter.'"

"When we look up and see the sky black with geese," said Marteel, "we glad they go south to keep warm."

It was very quiet in the narrow willow-lined bayou. Sometimes a blue heron or a snowy egret went flashing by. Sometimes a few coots or mud-hens ran over the surface of the water, before rising on the wing. Idly Suzette leaned over and picked a few water hyacinth blossoms. A mother duck, alarmed at human intrusion, began to squawk and trail one wing through the water, warning her young ones, who scurried off into the tall reeds along the shore.

Then all was quiet again. Once Suzette looked up and saw that the stream ahead was full of logs. She thought to herself that the flood must have uprooted a great many trees, but unheeding, went on gathering the blue hyacinth clusters. Marteel sat still, her eyes closed, her paddle idle. Soon the pirogue drifted closer.

Suddenly through the silence, violence came. A shot exploded, and the ducks splashed up from the water, with loud honking clatter and wing-whirring. One of the logs came to life, moved swiftly toward the pirogue and struck it with terrific force. At the same moment, the girls saw figures moving rapidly along shore, and heard them shouting. Then, as suddenly, a skiff appeared among the logs and in it stood Papa Jules, with a long-handled curved hook in his hand.

"GIT OUT!" he yelled. "W'at you girls doin' here? Takin' a nap? That 'gator's wounded, he'll turn your boat over! GIT OUT!"

Quickly Marteel took up her paddle and pushed the pirogue through the mass of floating logs which were not logs at all but moving alligators. In a moment it was at a safe distance.

"Marteel!" shouted Papa Jules. "W'y you not help me today? W'y you come and chase away the biggest one when I go after him?"

Marteel did not answer but paddled on.

"W'y you not tell me those logs, they alligator?" demanded Suzette. "W'y you take me on alligator hunt, when you know I not want to go?"

"Still 'fraid of alligator?" asked Marteel, smiling.

"No," said Suzette. "I gettin' used to 'em."

Soon after they reached the mound, the men came back from the hunt. They had three large alligators and one small one in the skiff. Suzette watched the skinning. The skin was loosened by cutting down the backbone, around the feet and down the center of the tail, then it was lifted off with one good pull. Salt was rubbed on the hide before it was rolled up, the heavy scaly part being thrown away. Marteel cleaned up afterwards, called the chickens and fed them some of the refuse.

That evening, she was more helpful than usual. She

seemed happy because Suzette was there. Maman was busily occupied, re-packing clothing in the hut, so Marteel offered to cook supper. She built up a good fire, let the blaze die down to hot coals and soon had two large covered skillets sizzling.

"W'at you cookin'?" asked Suzette, in surprise. She could not remember having seen Marteel cook before. "You not know how to cook, you!" Suzette gave her a light kick with her foot. "You look like one ole squaw,

bending over the fire. That the way the Injuns do it? W'at you cookin' anyhow?"

"Fish!" said Marteel, with a grin. "Good feesh. Bes' kind you ever ate."

Suzette peered over and looked in when Marteel lifted the covers.

"It look nice and purty," she said, "and it smell good. W'at kinda fish is it?"

"Me, I tell you after you eat it," said Marteel, scrambling hastily to get out the plates.

Tante Celéste came over from Nonc Moumout's hut for supper. The fish was delicious, very sweet and tender. Everybody agreed that Marteel was a good cook. Maman said she was so good she might help a little oftener. As soon as the plates were empty, Suzette demanded, "Now tell us w'at kind o' fish it was, Marteel."

With a flash of white teeth in her brown face, Marteel cried out: "Alligator tail!"

Then she got up and ran.

It was well she did, for everyone was furious. The fish did not taste so good now, but the two skillets were empty and there was nothing that could be done about it.

"W'at in the name o' sense," cried Maman, "do that Sabine mean . . . feedin' us alligator tail!"

Eulalie ran to get water to wash out her mouth. "Me, I eat *snake* 'fore I eat alligator!" she cried.

Tante Celéste put her hand to her head. "Me, I feel

sick!" she wailed. "Me, I feel like I gonna die quick. That awful feesh, I gonna taste it to my dying day!"

Papa Jules laughed and roared. "Marteel, she smarter'n I t'ink. Me, I et alligator once when I was leetle—guess it all right, it never killed me nohow."

Ambrose was very angry. "If she not a girl, me, I fight her!" he shouted. "Me, I say I won't never touch it, now she made me, that wicked leetle Sabine . . ." He looked at Papa Jules and began to laugh too.

Jacques ran after Marteel and waved a big stick at her. Little Noonoo and Joseph danced around, shouting: "We et alligator tail! We et alligator tail!"

Marteel went off in the pirogue. She waited till things had quieted down a little before she came back. Suzette met her at the water's edge.

"You t'ink we all pigs and chickens, you feed us alligator tail to fatten us up?" she demanded.

Marteel said nothing.

"Was that alligator tail for true?"

"Yes," answered Marteel, with a grin.

"W'at you feed it to us for?"

"So you say it *good!*" laughed Marteel.

"It *not* good!" cried Suzette, stamping her foot, "and you a bad girl, Marteel."

Suzette stepped into the pirogue to go back to Grandmère, and all the way home, said not a word to the Indian girl. When they reached the house, Grandmère was sitting

on a chair on the front gallery, which she had cleaned and scrubbed. Marteel came up and sat hunched on the bottom step while Suzette scolded.

"Marteel, she been takin' a ride on the 'gator's back?" asked Grandmère.

But Suzette did not even smile. "We gonna clean up this house," she said, sternly. "First we shovel out all the dead snakes and eels and fish. Then we shovel out the dirt and scrub it clean. You gonna help. Hear me?"

Marteel nodded, looking very repentant.

"Time you stop your wild ways, stop playin' all day, and do a leetle work," added Suzette.

Grandmère looked from one girl to the other, puzzled. "Poor Marteel," she said. "She done somet'ing bad, yes?"

"Yes," said Suzette. "She cook supper for us on the camp-fire and she call it feesh and . . ."

"The fish, it not good?" asked Grandmère.

"Yes . . . I mean NO!" cried Suzette. "It en't no feesh at all, it . . ."

"ALLIGATOR TAIL!" cried Marteel, doubling over with laughter.

Grandmère laughed heartily. "How terrible!" she said.

"She gotta clean up all this mud," Suzette repeated.

"Me, I will!" said Marteel, meekly.

Then she looked up with a sparkle in her eye. "Me, I like mud," she said. "Mud, it feel good on my toes!"

CHAPTER THIRTEEN

Good Friends Again

"A little piece of pepper
In the gumbo made with fish,
That a thing that's good—
That a thing delic' !"

SUZETTE sang the foolish little rhyme over and over. She and Marteel were on Papa Jules' wharf, and Felix, Theo and Jacques were on Nonc Moumout's. The bayou waters beneath, restless always, lapped gently against the shore.

"Me, I ketch river shrimp," announced Suzette. "Ma-man, she make jambalaya for supper."

She threw a basketful of small mashed crabs overboard for bait. After waiting about ten minutes, she opened her cast-net, threw it in out-spread, and lowered it into the bayou waters. But when she pulled the net up again, it held only a few crabs and mullets.

"No shrimp!" she cried, crossly. "That ole gar-fish, he been here. He got a nest under the grass and lilies round here somewhere. Nonc Moumout, he say the gar-fish break down all his nets, steal his bait and eat all his bunch of fish after he ketch 'em. Nasty ole gar-fish!

"Me, I gonna ketch that ole gar-fish," cried Felix, from the next wharf.

"We all ketch gar-fish!" announced Jacques. "We get lines and hooks and bait . . ."

"If only Papa Jules was here," sighed Suzette, "or Ambrose. Marteel, you might help me ketch him." She looked down at the Indian girl who did not move. "Me, I do it myself then." She folded up her cast-net and taking it with her, ran back to the shed. She brought out a heavy rope line with a large three-pronged hook attached. "You gotta have a strong iron hook, Papa say, 'count of all inside their mouth is bones."

"Gar-fish got plenty teeths, too," shouted Felix. "They bite peoples and eat 'em up. That w'y they call 'em alligator-gar. They're mean like alligators too."

"Well, this one en't gonna eat nobody up," said Suzette, busily fastening her line and baiting her hook.

"En't you gonna help me, you lazy t'ing?" she demanded angrily. "You gonna let this one ole gar-fish eat up all our crab and all our fish and all our shrimp when Papa Jules and Ambrose they en't here to do nothin' 'bout it?"

Marteel said nothing and did not move.

Suzette threw her hook into the water and tied the other end of the rope line to one of the wharf posts. Then she sat down to wait.

It seemed strange without Papa Jules at home. Suzette

remembered how it all came about. One day after the flood
was over and they had moved back into the house again,
Maman, Papa and Eulalie had dressed up in their best
clothes. Maman had struggled into her corset with many
moans and groans. Papa put on a stiff celluloid collar and
a bright red tie, and Eulalie her dotted swiss with the blue
sash. Together they left for Nonc Lodod's.

They stayed a long time. When they returned, Maman
rushed indoors quickly and took off her corset, to be comfortable again, and Eulalie changed her dress. Then the
exciting news came out. Papa Jules was to go shrimping in
the Gulf with Nonc Lodod on one of his luggers. And not
long after that, in early August, Suzette had watched the
shrimp luggers sail down the bayou. They all hoped that
Papa Jules would make his fortune.

> "A little piece of pepper
> In the gumbo made with fish,
> That a thing that's good—
> That a thing delic' !"

Suzette sang the silly song over and over. Marteel rested
with her chin in the palm of her hand. The boys were pulling crabs to pieces to use for bait, when suddenly Felix
yelled, "She's got 'im!"

Marteel looked lazily up to see Suzette pulling hard on
her line. Something very heavy was on the end of it. Suzette untied the line, took hold of the post to steady herself

and pulled harder. The line was very heavy.

"Marteel . . ." she wailed. "En't you gonna help me?"

Marteel's eyes brightened, but still she did not move.

"She got a gar-fish! Suzette's got a gar-fish!" cried the boys.

Like a flash, Marteel was on her feet and her hands on the rope next to Suzette's, both pulling with all their strength. The boys came running over and pulled too.

"Papa Jules . . . I mean Nonc Lodod . . . I mean Nonc Moumout . . . come quick!" called Suzette.

A great spiky head, showing a mouth, well-lined with teeth, in which the hook was inserted, moved slowly up out of the water at the end of the rope line.

Just then a bicycle, which was coming leisurely down the bayou path, stopped suddenly and the owner's cheerful whistling stopped too. *"Tonnerre m'emporte!"* exclaimed the young man. "W'at do I see!"

The next instant he too had his hands on the rope. A few moments later, a seven-foot gar-fish lay on the wharf.

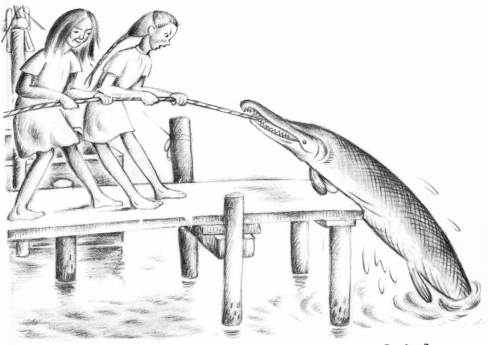

Suzette backed away, her eyes popping. "Me, I ketched . . . a gar-fish!" she said, feebly.

"You sure did!" answered the young man.

"W'at I gonna do with it?" she cried. "It en't no good to eat, and if I flip it back in the by'a, it gonna eat up all Nonc Moumout's feesh and all our crab and river shrimp."

For answer, the young man picked up an axe and knocked the huge fish on the head. "Now he won't eat nobody's fish," he said, quietly.

"Oh . . . thank you for helping me," said Suzette, breathless.

"It not'ing, that. Me, I was stopping here anyway."

"Papa Jules and Nonc Lodod and Ambrose, they all gone away to the Gulf," Suzette went on, "and Nonc Moumout, he not come quick when I call!"

"A good t'ing I happen along then," said the youth.

"Marteel, she try, but she not strong enough either . . ."

"Hardly," said the young man, "even with the boys helping. That fish probably weighs more than you do."

Suzette looked up to see who she was talking to. "Oh!" she gasped, in dismay. "Jean Broussard! I en't supposed . . . to talk . . . to you!"

"You en't supposed to ketch gar-feesh, either, are you?"

"No," said Suzette, "but there en't nobody else to . . ."

"So you did it yourself," said Jean Broussard. "You got spunk and me, I like you. You remind me of your sister, Lala. By the way, where is she?"

"Me, I don't know," said Suzette, lamely. "In the house, I guess."

She forgot her astonishment over the gar-fish as she stared, open-mouthed, at Jean Broussard. Leaving his bicycle beside the front gate, he strode boldly into the yard, walked up the front steps and knocked on the front door. Eulalie, dressed in her dotted swiss, as if expecting him, opened it. Jean Broussard entered and the door closed behind him.

"Your ole gar-fish, he won't eat crab and shrimp no more," said Marteel.

But Suzette did not hear. She flew round to the back door. She flew into Maman's arms and scattered to the floor all the potatoes she was peeling.

"Maman!" she cried, in a shocked whisper. "You know who is visitin' with Lala right now in the front room, in this very house?"

Maman showed no surprise, nor did Grandmère sitting beside her, calmly shelling beans.

"Maman! It Jean Broussard!" Suzette's heart pounded wildly. "Maman! You en't *let* him come, while Papa Jules he gone away?"

Slowly and deliberately Maman nodded her head. Then she explained.

"You 'member the day when Papa and Maman, they go visit Nonc Lodod to fix up 'bout Papa goin' shrimpin' on Nonc Lodod's boat? You 'member Lala went along too?

Well, Nonc Lodod, he had Claude Broussard there and Claude Broussard and Papa Jules, they talk . . ."

" 'Bout the bullet in his back?"

"No—the bullet it en't even mention' that day," said Maman, smiling. "Your Papa, he forgot all 'bout it. They talk 'bout Jean and Lala, and 'fore we come home, Papa Jules he tell Claude Broussard they can be friends."

"And Papa Jules, he say Jean he can come here to visit Lala in the front room?" asked Suzette, in astonishment.

"Yes, that just w'at Papa Jules he say," said Maman. "Then they shook hands, Papa Jules and Claude Broussard."

"Papa Jules shook hands with Claude Broussard?" cried Suzette, incredulous.

"Yes," said Maman. "Now they good friends again, like they used to be long ago."

Suzette was silent for a few moments to take it all in. A great turmoil went on inside her and it took her a while to get used to the new idea. She remembered Mardi Gras and how seeing Jean and Lala together was all just a part of the fun. She remembered the days long ago when Elise and Ellen Elaine had been her best friends. Then she was glad that Papa was not mad at Claude Broussard any more.

Maman took Suzette in her arms and gave her a big hug and so did Grandmère. If Maman and Grandmère approved, it must be all right.

When Jean Broussard came out the front door, Suzette

was waiting by the gate. She looked up at him.

"You find Lala?" she asked.

Jean nodded. "She was waitin' for me."

"My Papa Jules, he not mad at your Papa no more," said Suzette. "Elise and Ellen Elaine, they mad at me?"

"No," said Jean. "They never been mad at you at all."

"They talk to me now? A Broussard can talk to a Durand, yes?"

"Yes," said Jean. "All that foolishness, it over now. Lala and me, we make an end to it. Our Papas, they shake hands again, and they let their children speak together again."

As he started off on his bicycle, whistling happily, Suzette felt a wave of happiness come over her.

Jean looked back. "He was a good fighter, yes?"

At first she couldn't think what he meant. Then she remembered the gar-fish. Rushing to the kitchen again, she announced her catch, and Maman and Grandmère hurried out to the wharf to see it.

"Ugh! Ugly ole t'ing!" cried Maman. "Bad as a shark."

The gar-fish's nose was long and pointed. His back was covered with tough diamond-shaped scales, and his tail was flat. His head resembled an alligator's, but his body was that of a fish.

"W'at I gonna do with him, now I ketch him?" asked Suzette.

"Nonc Moumout, he skin him," said Grandmère. "He slice the good meat in thin slabs and salt and dry it. The rest he use for crab and fish bait."

Nonc Moumout came at last and towed the fish away.

That evening, Suzette washed herself with care and brushed and combed her hair. She put on a fresh clean dress. She washed and combed Marteel and Marteel put on a clean dress too. Together they started out.

"Papa Jules, he not mad at Claude Broussard no more," Suzette explained. "Now a Durand can talk to a Broussard, yes."

Marteel, walking beside her, said nothing.

Elise and Ellen Elaine were sitting on the bayou bench in front of their house. At the back of the bench a china-

ball tree, covered with hanging clusters of hard, green berries, thrust up its stiff branches like an umbrella. A bright red lizard crawled across the top board, and the girls were poking at it with small twigs.

> "Lizzie, Lizzie,
> Show me your blanket
> Or I'll kill you!"

cried Elise. The lizard immediately puffed out the bright red fold beneath his chin.

"Now you don't have to kill him," said Suzette.

"No," said Elise, looking up with a smile.

The little animal scampered off onto the tree trunk and disappeared.

"Me, I ketched a gar-fish," announced Suzette, casually.

"Jean, he tole us," said Elise. "You must be purty strong."

"Marteel, she help me first," Suzette explained. "But we couldn't never have pull' it up if Jean he not come when he came."

"Jean, he say it a whopper," said Elise.

"Jean, he thay it the biggeth gar-fith he ever thee!" lisped Ellen Elaine.

Suzette basked in the warmth of friendship. It was just as if Elise and she had always stayed friends. The long silence made no difference at all.

Beulah Bergeron and Doreen Dugas came strolling along.

"Chere chandelle!" cried Beulah, stopping suddenly in her tracks and pointing with her finger. "Look w'at I see! Suzette Durand talkin' to Elise Broussard!"

"Ma bonté!" cried Doreen, staring. "The world, it comin' to an end. A Durand has speak to a Broussard!"

Beulah and Doreen came nearer.

Suzette pulled Elise close beside her on the bench and Ellen Elaine close on the other side. "We good friends again," she announced.

"Suzette, your Papa he en't mad at Claude Broussard no more?" asked Beulah, unbelieving.

Suzette shook her head.

"Elise, your Papa he en't mad at Jules Durand no more?" asked Doreen, astonished.

Elise shook her head.

Beulah and Doreen sat down on the outer ends of the bench. "Tell us about it," they said.

Suzette was in the middle of the story when Tante Céleste walked up. She looked as if she were coming from Pére Eugéne's store, for she had a basket on her arm, filled with groceries.

"Suzette!" she cried, in astonishment. "W'at you doin'? Holdin' arms with two Broussards and talkin' to 'em when your Papa, he forbid you to? En't you shame' yourself, to disobey your Papa like this just when he gone away and can't watch you? Me, I gonna tell your Maman and I reckon she take a strap to you. . . ."

Suzette lifted her chin. "My Maman, she don't never take no strap to me for not'ing, Tante Céleste."

"She do it this time, sure, when I tell her." Tante Céleste smiled as if in delight at the prospect.

"My Maman she tell me to put on a fresh clean dress," said Suzette, with pride. "And Marteel too."

"W'at for?" asked Tante Céleste, puzzled.

"To wear when I come visit Elise and Ellen Elaine," said Suzette. "She tell me to visit them. She tell me I can speak to any Broussard any time I want to."

"But even if your Maman she crazy, w'at your Papa gonna say when he come back from shrimpin' and find out?"

"My Papa, he be ver' please'," said Suzette.

"Please'? You make one big mistake, Susu. Angry is w'at you mean," said Tante Céleste.

"He be ver' please'," Suzette went on, "that Jean Broussard, he come every week to visit Lala in the front room by our house."

"He visit Lala?" gasped Tante Céleste. "In the front room?" Clearly this was more serious than sitting holding hands on the bayou bench. Her eyes opened wide.

Suzette nodded. "Yes, 'cause Papa en't mad at Claude Broussard no more."

"They on kissin' terms now? Jules, he has forgot the bullet in his back, I suppose!" cried Tante Céleste.

"Yes," said Suzette. "It not a bullet at all. It only rheumatiz. That w'at Maman been tellin' him all along. Papa, he believe it too and he go shake hands with Claude Broussard just 'fore they go off shrimpin' together on Nonc Lodod's boat. And when they come back, there gonna be a wedding. One Durand and one Broussard, they gonna git married!''

Elise's and Ellen Elaine's faces broke into broad smiles. Beulah and Doreen smiled happily, too.

"Married, bah!" cried Tante Céleste. "How your Papa pay for a wedding when he can't even pay for his groceries, when he already got big debt by Pére Eugéne? Your Papa, he never no good to make a living for his family."

Suzette's cheeks flushed. She stood up and clenched her fists at her side. It was hard to keep on being polite to Tante Céleste, but she knew she must. "My Papa, he gonna help Nonc Lodod bring home a big catch of shrimp and make plenty money so Lala can have her wedding. My Maman, she tell me so. They gettin' ready."

"Huh! They won't git married," scoffed Tante Céleste. "Your Maman, she keep hopin' for the best, but it never come. Your Papa, he keep hopin' for a boat of his own but he never git it. Somet'ing it all the time happen—a bullet in his back, rheumatiz, bad weather, bad luck—all the time the same ole story."

Suzette turned cold all over.

"This time, it gonna be different, Tante Céleste," she said, in a feeble voice.

Tante Céleste walked on, swinging her basket at her side. Suzette looked after her and a tear rolled down her cheek. Marteel, who had sat on the ground through it all and said nothing, jumped up suddenly and put her arm round Suzette's waist.

"Come," said Beulah. "We go by Père Eugène and buy candy balls and sugar hearts. My Papa, he give me six pennies—enough for all."

The girls started off, their arms entwined. As Suzette walked with them, in her heart a great fear began to poke up its ugly head.

Would Papa Jules' catch be a good one?

CHAPTER FOURTEEN

Home at Last

IT WAS evening along the bayou. After supper, Grandmère and Maman came out to the bayou bench in front of the house. The air was close and hot for October. There was little breeze to stir the leaves of the chinaball tree, and only a soft, gurgling movement of gentle waves against the shore.

Joseph and Jacques built a smudge fire at the edge of the levee and kept feeding it with branches and twigs, and smothering it with damp weeds. The smoke blew lazily off the bayou and hung in the still air, discouraging mosquitoes.

As Grandmère began to talk, the children crowded round and listened with respect—all but Marteel. She went off by herself to the end of the wharf and sat there, cross-legged and hunch-backed, fishing.

"Papa Jules, he eat only one good meal a day when he out shrimping," said Grandmère, "after his breakfast of black coffee and hard tack. The men, they work hard from dawn till nightfall. When a showing of shrimp appear, out go the anchor lines and down come the sails. The men, they jump in the skiffs and go out to lay a quarter of a mile

circular net or seine around the school of shrimp. Then, to
haul in the seine, when it full of shrimp—how hard the
men gotta pull! It hard work, that!"

"Papa Jules, he come home again soon?" asked Suzette.

The question was in everyone's mind, but Grandmère
did not answer it. "Two boats, they work together," she
went on. "Your Papa, he go on one out to sea to haul in the
seine. Nonc Lodod, he use the other for ice, to pack the
shrimp so they will keep. At night, the men eat a big
supper, and when the luggers come in to some port along
the Gulf, go to bed in their bunks, dead tired. . . ."

"Jules, he gone six week now," said Maman, sadly, "and
we never know w'at happen out there in the Gulf. And
Ambrose—it hard work for a boy."

"Ambrose, he strong enough to stand it," said Grandmère. "Out there in the Gulf, the sun it shine, the wind it
blow, the black clouds and storms they come, the waves
dash high and lift the boats up and down—then the storm
it pass and all is calm again. The same t'ings happen before
to all the other Durands when they went to sea.

"It hard work, yes, but exciting, too, the excitement a
man loves when he wins his daily bread at terrific odds.
Even when the sea it against him, he still the master, he
win in the end."

Suzette, leaning against Grandmère's shoulder, looked
up. "He bring home a good catch then?" But again, the
question was not answered.

So intent was the little group under the chinaball tree, they had not seen or heard a sailing lugger coming slowly up the bayou. Only the Indian girl, alone on the wharf, raised her eyes and watched it come closer and closer, its orange-colored sail half-hauled.

As Grandmère's voice droned on, Marteel saw the men on board tugging at the ropes. She saw the sail fall to the deck, catching highlights from the setting sun. The lugger slid closer now, then it shivered and with a jolt, stood still. A man on board seized a "gaff" or push-pole and leaned over, trying to push the boat free from the mud-flat on which it was apparently stuck.

Marteel's eyes brightened. She glanced toward the group under the chinaball tree, but they were still listening to Grandmère. Marteel smiled to herself. Then she saw that the lugger was grounded. She frowned as she listened to the men's voices.

The man on the deck jabbed the push-pole into the mud-flat again and again. The boat swerved slightly and the pole went deeper into a hole. The man lost his balance and fell overboard.

Marteel jumped to her feet. The sun was gone now, but her eyes were sharp even in darkness. She saw and heard no motion in the water, she saw no figure climb up on the levee bank—the man had not come ashore. She saw the other men, five or six figures still busy on the deck and she knew they had not noticed the man's plight. What had happened to him? Marteel stared intently. Only for a moment did she hesitate. Then she dove into the water and swam as fast as she could toward the boat.

"W'at dat?" cried Jacques. "I hear a big splash."

Suzette jumped to her feet and pointed. "Marteel! She not fishing on the wharf, she swimming . . ."

"Look! A boat! A sailing lugger—a shrimper home from the Gulf!" cried the boys.

They all ran down to the wharf.

They stared at the lugger, dimly outlined in the increasing darkness, as if they had never seen it before. Yes, it was Nonc Lodod's lugger, but somehow it looked ghostly and unreal. It was as if it had been away so long they had forgotten its graceful lines, its size, its shape. And why had it stopped down-stream?

"W'at the matter?" cried Maman, putting her trembling hand to her lips. "Somet'ing it has happen' to Lodod's lugger."

"Never mind!" said Grandmère, putting her hand on Maman's arm. "It back at last. Our Jules, he home again."

"It Papa Jules!" cried Suzette, shrilly. "Papa Jules, he back!"

The two women and the children saw figures in the water moving slowly toward the shore.

"I see a man's head in the by'a!" cried Suzette, panic-stricken.

They all ran down the bayou path. They came in time

to see a dripping, unconscious man hauled up on the bank at their feet. Before Marteel had reached shore, pulling her heavy burden, a skiff had come up beside her, Claude Broussard had climbed out to help her.

Suzette got there first. She knelt and with her skirt wiped the water from her father's face and eyes. But Marteel pushed her roughly back. She raised the limp body, lifting the arms to let water pour forth from the lungs. Grandmère, with a prayer on her lips, helped. Maman fell to her knees and cried and moaned: "He dead! Jules, my Jules, he dead!"

The men from the lugger came quickly ashore, Nonc Lodod and the others. They picked Jules Durand up and carried him along the bayou path and into his home. Yes, it was true, he was home again from the Gulf.

Suzette repeated it over and over, to all the neighbors who came hurrying in that night and all the next day. He was home from the Gulf. He fell overboard and knocked his head against the boat. Marteel swam to his rescue and pulled him, unconscious, to shore. Now he was resting quietly, but he neither opened his eyes nor spoke. It was a different home-coming from what she had expected.

Nonc Lodod told the story of the successful voyage, the largest catch of shrimp they had ever brought in. He laid it all to the fact that he had the two best men from the bayou on his crew—Jules Durand and Claude Broussard. He talked briskly of all their adventures and mishaps,

their storms and fair weather and best of all, of the heavy
load of shrimp, which meant prosperity for all.

Suzette listened, along with Maman and Grandmère,
but somehow the big catch meant nothing now. All desire
for silk dresses, a house-boat and phonograph like Thérèse's
was gone. There was only one thing that mattered—that
Papa Jules should wake up and speak again.

Nonc Lodod went on: "Jules, he gonna take over my
old lugger for his own, as part of his share from the voyage.
It not a bad boat and Jules, he say he like to have it."

A boat of his own for Papa Jules at last! But would he
ever be able to give it the coat of paint it needed, would
he ever be able to sail it again to the Gulf? A tear stole
down Suzette's cheek.

Days passed and Papa Jules grew slowly better. One
day he spoke a few words and after that his progress was
more rapid. After a while he was able to have visitors.
Claude Broussard came often, his best friend again, as long
before the unfortunate shooting-match. Tante Céleste
and the other aunts and uncles came, Père Eugène, and
many others. To all of them Papa Jules told the story of
Marteel's rescue.

"Without that Indian girl, me, I'd be lyin' on the bottom of the by'a this minute!" he always added, with a
chuckle.

Papa Jules never thanked Marteel directly for saving his
life, nor did Maman, Grandmère, or any other member of

the family. They would have been ashamed to voice their thoughts in words. There were other ways they could show their thanks to the Indian girl and did so. Marteel was accepted as one of the family as she had never been before. All doubt and suspicion were completely removed. In one way after another during the many months she had persisted in staying with them, she had proven her own worth and her devoted loyalty. Now she was one of them and belonged to them. Suzette felt it and knew that Marteel felt it too.

Yes, it was good to hear Papa Jules' voice again. Suzette was happy as never before. It was better still when he was well enough to be up again. The happiest day of all was when Papa Jules made his first trip to Père Eugène's store and returned with a large package in his arms.

With great ceremony, Papa Jules undid all the wrappings and placed on the kitchen table a phonograph with a blue and gold horn shaped like a huge morning-glory! Papa Jules put one of the records on, set it going, and the music machine began to play. Then he took firm hold of Maman Clothilde's waist and the two danced gaily round the kitchen, while the rest of the family looked on, admiring and clapping and stamping their feet! Yes, that was such a happy day, it seemed impossible there could ever be a happier. But if there ever was, it was the day of Lala's wedding to Jean Broussard.

The wedding began early and lasted late. There was an

abundance of food for all the relations of both families
and for all the bayou neighbors. Arsene Cheramie brought
his fiddle, Alcide Brunet his accordion, the furniture was
pushed back against the walls and everybody danced—
even Grandmère, to the applause of the crowd.

At nightfall the entire wedding party moved along the
bayou path to a new little house which had been built in
Claude Broussard's yard. There, Eulalie and Jean mounted

the steps alone. They had not been inside before, and as Jean struck a match, Eulalie gave a cry of happiness. All the neighbors had given presents to furnish the house— furniture and clothing and cooking utensils. There was even food waiting to be cooked by the bride, as she began her new life.

Grandmère and Maman shed happy tears as they walked home again. Then morning came and the wedding was a thing of the past.

Not long after that, a strange man came one day to see Papa Jules. His skin was dark, his hair long and black and he wore a mixed lot of curious clothes. He said his name was Sabine Joe.

"You want to see Marteel?" asked Papa Jules.

Suzette stood by. "You come to take her away?" she cried, suddenly fearful.

"No," said the man, hurriedly. "Don't call her. I don't want to see her, don't never want to see her again."

Laboriously he opened a bundle he carried. He brought out a cape of wool on which bright-colored beads in intricate design had been painstakingly sewn. It was worn and old, but very beautiful.

"Long ago, the People-of-the-Rising-Sun, they go to the Indian mound on Feast days. They dance there from the rising to the setting of the sun," said Sabine Joe. "Long ago, the Houma women wear beaded capes when they dance. Marteel's great-great-grandmother, she wear this cape."

"Then Marteel, she got a great-great-grandmother, after all?" asked Suzette, astonished.

"W'y yes, of course," said Sabine Joe. "Her name, it Queen Nuyu'n. She wear this cape, she a great woman of the Houmas."

"Where the cape been all this time?" asked Papa Jules.

"Ole woman, she keep it," said Sabine Joe, sullenly.

"W'at ole woman?" asked Papa Jules.

"Me, I know. The ole squaw w'at poked the burning splinters in Marteel's back," answered Suzette. "The one w'at make medicine to . . ."

Sabine Joe frowned. "Ole squaw dead now," he announced.

"Marteel's grandmother?" asked Papa Jules.

"No," said Sabine Joe. "Marteel's mother and grandmother, they long time dead. Ole squaw mother to Sabine Joe, me." He pointed to himself. "We take care of Marteel after her mother die. Injuns all get white man's sickness and die off like flies. Marteel was left with nobody to take care of her but us."

"And how you take care of her!" cried Suzette, indignant. "You en't make her no home, you en't give her no bed to sleep in, you en't cook her no meals, you give her only rags to wear. And w'y, I wanta know w'y the ole squaw all the time hurt her?"

"Hurt her?" grunted Sabine Joe, with a shrug of his shoulders. "That the Injun way to make a girl grow up strong."

"Yes," said Papa Jules, "the Indian women have to be strong so they can wait on the lazy men."

"That right," said Sabine Joe, "that the Injun way. Ole woman before she die, she tell me to bring cape to Marteel." He handed it out to Papa Jules. "It belong to Queen Nuyu'n, her great-great-grandmother. She buried in the Indian mound at the Bayou des Oies along by Chief Shulu-shumon. The Chief and his queen, they both buried there . . . at the top of that big pile o' clam shells."

"At the Indian mound?" gasped Suzette.

Papa Jules grew thoughtful. "We all the time knew it was an Indian burying ground. Plenty arrowheads and broken bits of pottery and utensils been found there."

"Marteel's great-great-grandparents, they buried at the Indian mound?" cried Suzette, incredulous.

"Yes, that's right," said Sabine Joe, staring stupidly. "W'at so strange about that?"

"Oh . . . not'ing . . ." said Suzette, lamely.

"The Indians, they here long before the white man," said Papa Jules. "Remember that, Susu. We thought the Durands owned that mound, we forget the Indians owned it first, built it themselves."

"You en't takin' Marteel away then?" asked Suzette, as the man started to go.

"No," said Sabine Joe. "She en't not'ing to me. Don't never want to see her again." He slouched down the steps.

Suzette ran after him. "W'at her name, Sabine Joe?"

"Whose name?"

"Marteel's. W'at her last name? She got one, en't she?"

"Oh yes—Dardar," said Joe. "Marteel Dardar."

"You don't never want Marteel Dardar back again?" asked Suzette. "The other savages, they don't want her?"

Sabine Joe shook his head and was gone.

Marteel Dardar was little disturbed by the news when Suzette told her, and quite unimpressed by her new name. She folded the old cape up carefully and tucked it under her moss mattress in the shed for safekeeping.

"Come, we make candles," she said. "Candles from the candleberry tree, they bring good luck."

"We carry them to the graveyard on All Saints' Day," said Suzette.

A year had passed and once more All Saints' Day came around. This time Marteel went proudly with the Durand family to the graveyard on the Indian mound. She and Suzette walked side by side, each carrying two blessed candles. The white painted crosses caught the light of the flickering candles of all the people in the long procession, as a gentle breeze blew in from the bayou.

Suzette knelt by Grandpère's and little Tit-tit's grave and said a prayer for each, with Marteel by her side. Then she walked with Marteel to the top of the Indian mound, where the Indian girl set down her candles and said an Indian prayer and chant for her great-great-grandparents who had once been chief and queen of the People-of-the-Rising-Sun, and for those unknown ancestors of hers who had built the great mound long before they ever saw a white man.

No one now disputed Marteel Dardar's right to worship at the Indian mound—the altar of her fathers.

Marteel and Suzette walked home from the graveyard arm in arm. When they reached the house, Papa Jules took Marteel in his arms and kissed her. Grandmère did the same. They wanted Marteel to know that she had found not only a name, not only worthy ancestors, but a home as well.

"Sabine Joe, he say the ole Injun squaw, she dead!" said Suzette, happily. "So you don't never have to go back to the Injuns again. You gonna stay here with us all the time now."

Marteel's white teeth flashed in her dark face.

"Marteel, white girl now," came the ready reply. "Suzette's sister, me."

Then she walked over to Maman, who took her in her arms and held her tight.

"How beautiful is my Maman!" said Marteel, softly.

THE END